"That's the one drawback of being a zombie—the damn hunger for human flesh, but I can live with that. Or not live with it, as is the case."

McMillian cracked his knuckles. "You're stupider than you look if you think you're gonna get a chance at bat for strike three."

Argus held his hands up to show they were empty. "This time, I just came to talk."

The dead man shrugged. "Sorry. Don't believe you. And even if I did, I need a snack. Regenerating all that flesh from when you shot me up yesterday made me real hungry. I can't be killed, but the cops can still lock me up. True, it'd take a hundred of 'em, but they got more than that. Mmm, should I start with white meat or dark? Maybe a little of both."

"I hate to ruin your dinner plans but I'm not on the menu today. Still, I hate to see you go hungry." Argus reached under his leather trench coat, but instead of pulling out a gun his hand emerged with a piece of rope. McMillian started to smile until he realized that tied to each end was a hand grenade. "I brought pineapple surprise." Before he had finished speaking, Argus had pulled the pins and threw the homemade bolo so it wrapped around the zombie's neck.

"Oh shit," said McMillian when he saw a grenade land near each ear.

PATRICK THOMAS

PADWOLF PUBLISHING INC.
WWW.PADWOLF.COM
www.facebook.com/Padwolf

WWW.PATTHOMAS.NET
WWW.MURPHYS-LORE.COM
www.facebook.com/PatrickThomasAuthor

CHOICES, SMALL SCALE WAR, and ACT OF CONTRITION
were originally published in the limited edition
SOUL FOR HIRE: 3 SHOTS TO THE HEART

A BULLET FOR THE DEAD Was originally published in
EMPTY GRAVES

CUTE AS A BUTTONwas originally published in NIGHTCAPS

Book edited by John L. French

Cover photo by Chris M. LaBree
Cover model Frank Thon
Cover Design by Roy Maurtisen

10-digit ISBN 1-890096-72-5, 13 digit ISBN 978-1-890096-72-4
Printed in the USA
First Printing

For Thomas Karwacki
for bringing Argus to life on the screen

With special thanks to
Chris M. LaBree
Frank Thon
and
Ron Rogell
for
helping him.

"Killing is only a solution, it's never the answer."
-Vince Argus, Soul for Hire

CHOICES

"You've got a bright and cheery place here, especially for a house of death."

Indignation welled up within the doctor and threatened to spew out at the comment. As a physician, Dr. Steven Merrill was usually treated with deference. Whenever he wasn't, a few well-placed snide remarks usually put the offender back in his place. But every iota of common sense screamed at him that it would be truly dangerous to try this with this fellow. If even half of what he had heard about Vince Argus was true, he was standing before a very deadly and dangerous man. Truth be told, very few people made him nervous. Argus made him sweat. There wasn't just one thing that sparked the perspiration, it was more a combination of factors. Some the doctor could recognize, others he struggled to ignore. Regardless, he did not want to antagonize this man.

Despite his unspoken pledge to allow the comment to slide, the ensuing silence begged to be filled. Under other circumstances, Merrill would have easily toughed it out, making his conversational opponent uncomfortable until *he* spoke up to fill the void. Face to face with Argus, Merril broke first and ended the discomforting silence

"Don't tell me you're pro-life?"

Argus chuckled. "Why's that?"

"Because of your…" Too late, the doctor had realized what he was saying, but he was committed now. Best to be careful with his choice of words. He finally settled on "…profession."

"Because I'm a hitman I can't have the opinion that killing babies is wrong?" Argus asked sincerely.

The doctor became very nervous. The meeting was only happening because a pro-life fanatic was trying to kill him and he wanted to hire Argus to beat the assassin at his own game. It was only now that he realized that the killer he had invited to this private meeting could be his own. It was the perfect opportunity. If that was the case, Merrill was as good as dead. Forging ahead, Merrill decided to ignore that possibility as well as his common sense by arguing with the hitman.

"They're not babies, they're fetuses. It is better for them to be aborted than to come into families that can't support them or don't want them. Not that I have to defend or justify myself to you."

Argus definitely didn't like the elitist attitude and condescending tone that the doctor was using to present his case.

"I realize everyone isn't Catholic, but personally, I don't consider the Church wrong on this one. Regardless, I believe that everyone has the right to make their own choices, however wrong they may be. They just have to deal with the consequences when they die."

"You can't possibly be saying that you believe someone having an abortion is going to go to Hell."

Argus didn't exactly answer the question. "Hell is a very real place."

The doctor gave a snort. "You can't possibly believe in Hell. That's something religion invented to keep the masses in line."

Argus stood in silence, staring directly at him. Even though the hitman wore dark sunglasses, the doctor could tell he had not blinked the entire time. Rumors he had heard about Argus rose unbidden in his mind. Originally, he had chalked them up to folk tales told by the ignorant. Now, face to face with the man, he wasn't so sure.

Argus was allegedly the sole survivor of a mafia family massacre. People said he had sold his soul to the Devil to survive. What else he got as part of the deal varied, but one thing was clear – nobody had ever seen the man miss. Despite himself, the doctor started to wonder if what he had dismissed as so much hogwash could actually be true. Silently he chided himself for letting the intimidation he felt alter his better judgment.

"You're an atheist, Dr. Merrill?"

"More agonistic really, but do I lean more towards the atheist spectrum? Yes."

Argus raised his eyebrows and gave a subtle facial nod, the kind that indicated that he knew something that the doctor didn't and was amused by it. It annoyed Merrill.

"So, if you feel abortion is wrong, why would you agree to help me?" Dr. Merrill asked.

"Consider it a professional courtesy from one killer to another."

"Now wait just a minute! I've never killed anyone in my life."

"No, you've just never killed anybody after they've been born, but you kill fetuses for money. You're a hitman, like me. If you're doing it to make people's lives easier, so much the better. Looking at it that way, some would consider it noble. I'm not one of them. Killing's not noble, it's not good, but sometimes it has to be done. That reality shapes my life and yours. You can tell yourself and others differently, but we both know better. I'm not judging. Maybe you're right. Life is hard enough on a kid without being in a place where they are hated for just being born.

"And maybe having that kid would ruin the woman's life. Or maybe it's just a form of retroactive birth control. Like I said, it's all about choices and everyone is entitled to their own. Why don't we just move past this and have you tell me about your problem."

"You mean who I want you to kill?" the doctor said condescendingly, upset over Argus' accusations. The words stung, maybe because they were said without hate or judgment. Argus had struck a little close to home, although Dr. Merrill would never admit it to anyone, even himself.

"Well, I could just wound them, but that will cost you extra."

"Extra? Why?"

"A wounded person can testify, so there is more danger involved for me. I assumed you wanted someone dead. Give me the particulars and I'll decide if I take the hit."

The doctor was surprised. "You mean you turn jobs down? Even when people are offering to pay you?"

"Sure. I decide who should die by my hand."

"How do you decide who deserves to die?"

"That's not your concern. Now tell me who you want dead and why."

Alarm bells went off inside the doctor's head. "Wait a second. How do I know you're not wearing a wire?"

As soon as they had met, Argus had thoroughly searched Merrill, but it had been a one-way transaction.

"Would you like to frisk me? Would that make you feel better?" This time, it was Argus' turn to be condescending.

"Yes, it would."

Argus opened up his black trench coat. "Go ahead then."

The doctor moved in close to do just that and was stopped short, not by a sight but by a sound. An ominous click made him look down. Argus had an automatic cocked and pointed at the bottom of Merrill's chin. If he pulled the trigger, the back of the doctor's head, not to mention most of his brains, would be splattered along the office wall behind him.

All the doctor could say was, "What?"

"Letting anyone this close to me is dangerous. You can reach my guns. You can do something stupid. I chose to use a safeguard to make sure you don't make any mistakes."

The doctor could hear his heart pounding in his ears and his knees going weak. "I wasn't going to do anything to hurt you."

"Good, but it never hurts to be sure. Now hurry up."

The doctor wasn't as thorough as he would have preferred, but he was fairly certain there were no wires or recording devices on the hit man. There were a great many guns and at least one knife.

"Satisfied?" The doctor nodded numbly. With the wave of his hand, Argus indicated he was tired of waiting and the doctor should proceed with his story.

"Two months ago, a colleague of mine - Dr. Sheila Washington - received a threatening letter warning her she had one week to stop providing abortions or she would get a taste of her own medicine. A week to the day the letter arrived she was shot as she left her clinic, the same day the letter said it would happen. The bullet went through her skull. The coroner said it killed her instantly. Six days ago, I got the same letter."

"How do you know that it was the same letter?"

"Dr. Washington showed it to me and several others. There

aren't many of us left that do this work and we've become a close-knit community."

"So why contact me? Why not the police?"

"I already went to the police. So did Sheila. She played by the rules and they killed her anyway. The police are investigating and have no leads so there's no way for them to do anything until it's too late for me. I don't want to die."

"Nobody does."

"Will you do it?"

"As long as you agree to my conditions."

"What conditions? I just pay you the money, right?"

"That's not how I work. First off, my fee for this is four hundred thousand dollars."

"Four hundred thousand! That's outrageous, I can't afford that."

Argus smiled. "Sure you can. I had an associate of mine pull your tax returns for the last three years and check your accounts. You can get someone to kill another person for fifty bucks, but for something like this, you're better off with a professional. We don't come cheap. Of course, if it's too much, we can end this right here and we can each go home."

The doctor started to panic. It had taken the better part of the week to locate Argus. He would never find another person in his line of work before tomorrow. "No, I'll pay it."

"Good. I'll take it all in cash. Nothing bigger than a hundred by tomorrow morning."

The doctor thought about arguing that was too much too soon but decided against it. "Isn't half up front and half after the job customary?"

Argus smiled. "I don't work that way. I've never stiffed a client. Bad for business."

"Fine."

Argus reached into his pocket and did something that seemed very odd to the doctor. He pulled out a brass colored bullet. Things got even stranger for the doctor when he saw what was written on the bullet.

Dr. Steven Merrill.

"Why is my name engraved on that bullet?"

Argus knew the proper name for it was cartridge, that a bullet was what came out of the cartridge when it was fired. Argus also knew someone staring at it thought it was a bullet. To correct their language would distract from the point he was trying to make, so he also called it a bullet.

"This is the final part of how I do business. I have a code. If anything you told me is not true, if the person I'm to kill for you is not this murderer, then this bullet will be for you. I don't take being lied to lightly."

Argus handed him the bullet.

"Swear on that bullet that everything that you have told me is true, that there are no ulterior motives, that you have no idea who is threatening to kill you."

"I swear it on my life."

Argus shook his head and took off his sunglasses. "No. Swear it on this bullet, because if you're lying, this bullet will ensure that you never lie again."

Merrill looked into his eyes and saw orbs unlike any others he had ever encountered. Deep within, there was a darkness and a hardness. It was unnerving and frightening. It was as primal as prey standing before a predator. Merrill knew that even if he wanted to, he'd never be able to look into those eyes and lie.

The doctor swore. Argus held out his hand and the doctor gave back the high caliber name tag.

"Just so we're clear on the rest of the specifics, let me detail what your money is buying you. Tomorrow, I will be around all day. You will not leave the building until I say so. Anyone who tries to shoot you will be taken out by me," Argus said.

"What if they don't come tomorrow?" asked the nervous doctor.

"I'm willing to do the same thing every day for a week, but they'll come tomorrow."

"How do you know?"

"That's what they did with your doctor friend. They gave you one week and it's up tomorrow. Undoubtedly, you've shown that note to a lot of people by now. The police have analyzed it from handwriting to fingerprints and compared it to the note your dead friend got. If the note writer doesn't make good on their threat when they promised, their future threats are going to lose credibility. They're hoping to make abortion doctors quit out of a fear of dying. If people start thinking these threats aren't serious, these people will not be able to achieve their goals."

"What if they don't come on the days that you're here?"

Argus shrugged his shoulders. "Not my problem. But if it's something you're seriously worried about, we can always renegotiate when the time comes."

Biting on his lip, the doctor decided an internal debate and spoke. "What's to stop you tomorrow morning from running off with my money without doing anything?"

"Nothing but my reputation. If I did that to you, you would undoubtedly tell others, including the person who referred me to you. Word would get around and soon business would drop off for me. There are plenty of loose cannons out there who'll take you. I'm not one of them. You can choose to believe that or you can choose to not hire me."

"No, no. I still want to hire you," said the doctor.

Argus nodded. "I'll see you in the morning. Don't leave your house until I come get you."

Morning arrived all too quickly for the doctor. For an additional fee, Argus had arranged for a bulletproof limo to pick him up at home and take him to work. Argus sat across from him, again dressed in a long black trench coat and dark sunglasses. The hitman kept looking out the windows and sunroof for any sign of the would-be killer. Merrill had a leather computer bag which he held out.

"I'll get it from you later. Right now, I'm busy keeping you alive."

The limo pulled up a block away and stopped.

"Give me twenty minutes to make sure the clinic is still clear..."

"Still?"

"I've already been there last night and again this morning.

When I call, pull up at the front door," Argus said.

"There are usually protesters. I always sneak in the back."

"And whoever is trying to kill you probably knows that. The protesters are a good thing today. Think of them as cover, because they share the same beliefs as the person who wants you dead. With luck, they won't want to hit their ideological brethren with a stray shot. That would probably decrease the number of volunteers who protest in the future, which they wouldn't want."

Twenty minutes later at 7 A.M the limo pulled up in front of the clinic. Pro-life protestors were already picketing outside. There were only a half dozen, but the small numbers didn't deter their enthusiasm. In fact, the limo pulling up in front of the clinic seemed to excite them even more. The six, picket signs in hand, moved towards the limo yelling, screaming and banging on the windows and the roof. Inside, Merrill slid across the seat to the street side door. He briefly considered telling the driver to leave quickly, but then he saw Argus coming toward them from the clinic. Argus moved through the small group of angry protestors as if they were little more than ants until he reached the ring leader.

"Step away from the car please, sir," Argus said in a quiet, cool tone.

The man spun, ready to spurt his venom. The sight of the man facing stopped him short. The spurt caught in his throat. It took a moment to regain his equilibrium.

"That man is a murderer of unborn children."

"What's your point?" The casual remark caught the protestor off guard.

"He doesn't deserve to live."

"Are you going to kill him?" Argus asked.

"Somebody should. Hopefully, somebody will," the protestor shouted as if preaching to the crowd, hatred burning in his eyes and tainting his words. The rants were met with cheers.

"So why would it be okay to kill him?"

"He murders unborn babies."

"But murdering him would still be taking a life. Wouldn't that bring you down to his level?" Argus asked sincerely.

"It's just to smite those who do evil in the Lord's eyes."

"So, it's okay to kill someone if you don't agree with them. That's a very Christian attitude. What happened to turn the other cheek, judge not less ye be judged?"

"I don't have to explain myself to you," said the man.

"True, but you do have to back away from the car," Argus said, taking a step forward. The protestor reflexively took a step back. "Doesn't a court order regarding this ongoing protest state that you stay fifty feet back from here at all times?"

"There's no police here to enforce that."

Argus' smile was a cold and dark thing. "Actually, that would work out better for you than it would for me."

The two men made eye contact. The protestor was the first to break away, looking towards the ground. Doing his best to hide his chagrin and his fear, he motioned his fellow protestors back. While it wasn't the required fifty feet, it was more than enough for the doctor to get out of the limo.

Merrill handed the computer bag to Argus. Carrying that much money near the protesters was making the doctor even more nervous. Argus rolled his eyes at the amateur behavior.

"It's all there," Merrill whispered.

"It better be."

Merrill was impressed by how Argus had handled the protestors but was damned if he would admit it. "How do you know it's not one of them?"

"I don't, but none of them is carrying a gun. At the moment, the rooftops and other possible sniper holes are clear, but that could change. Stop yakking and move."

Dr. Merrill did as he was instructed and made it into the clinic without problems.

Most of the morning passed without incident. The doctor went about his business, most of which was regular OBGYN visits. All doors except the main entrance had been locked so no one could sneak in. After the death of Dr. Washington, Merrill had invested in a metal detector in hopes to reduce the threat of firearms or bombs making their way into the clinic. Argus just simply stepped around it when he entered, but he watched to make sure nobody else did. Periodically he would wander through the clinic, checking to make sure the doors and windows remained secure. As he was passing down one hallway he noticed one of the counselors and a teenage girl come out of one of the rooms. It was the girl who drew Argus' attention.

"Antonia?" Argus asked.

The girl looked up like a shivering deer caught in headlights. "Argus?"

"Excuse me sir, but our clients are kept confidential and…" Argus lifted up his hand, effectively silencing the woman.

"What are you doing here?" asked Antonia.

"I was about to ask you the same question. You're a long way from the neighborhood," Argus said.

Antonia realized it was obvious why she was there, so there was no reason denying it. "I'm pregnant. I came here for counseling, trying to decide what to do."

"Did you decide?"

"Not exactly, but after talking to Karen here, I realized I just can't get an abortion. I'm trying to decide between keeping the baby or giving it up for adoption. I just worry what everyone, especially my father, is going to say."

"These days being a single mother is nothing to be ashamed of," the counselor said.

"It is where we come from," Argus said to the woman. Turning back to Antonia he said, "Do you know who's the father?"

She nodded.

"Do you have five dollars?" asked Argus.

"Yes. Why?"

"I'd like to offer you my services."

The counselor, while not directly in the loop, had heard rumors about why this man was there. Karen was horrified about what she thought she heard. "Now wait a second…"

Argus ignored her. "I'd be more than happy to be with you when you tell your parents. I will also make sure that Jimmy lives up to his responsibilities in financially supporting his child if you choose to keep it."

"That would be so great. Thanks, Argus," Antonia said, pulling five dollars out of her jeans pocket and handing it over.

"Come see me in a couple of days. We'll figure out your options."

Antonia kissed Argus on the cheek and left. Despite herself, Karen approved of what Argus had done.

"That was very good of you," she said.

Argus nodded, accepting the complement. "That was good of you telling her all of her options."

"Just because we do abortions here, doesn't mean we push them. It may be pro-choice, but nobody is pro-abortion."

"Good."

"We try. I've been where she is."

"Did you have the child?"

"No."

"I'm sorry."

"So am I, but it was the right decision for me. It's not right for everybody."

An odd noise got Argus' attention. "What's that?"

"I don't know," Karen said.

Argus walked along the hall moving in the direction of the sound. It got louder. It sounded almost like a kitten. Seemed to be coming from behind a door marked *Medical Personnel Only*. Argus opened the door and went inside, despite Karen's protests that he wasn't allowed. The cries seemed to be coming from a red container which was designed to hold medical waste. Argus lifted the lid and what was inside horrified him. Picking it up, he kicked the surgery room door open and charged inside.

"What the hell is this?" Argus shouted.

Dr. Merrill was finishing up with a woman who was still under general anesthesia. He began to sweat.

"It's an aborted fetus."

"Then why the hell is she moving and breathing?" The doctor remained tongue-tied, unable to come up with an answer he felt the hitman would want to hear. "I thought third-trimester abortions were frowned upon."

"That fetus is barely twenty weeks. Third-trimester doesn't start until twenty-six."

"Don't treat me like an idiot, Doctor, just because of what I do for a living. If anything, you should be treating me with more respect because I'm intelligent enough to still be alive after doing it for all these years. I've studied anatomy and physiology to help what I do. This baby is more than twenty weeks. I'd say she's closer to thirty."

"Maybe twenty-eight," the doctor conceded reluctantly.

"In New York, it's illegal after 24 weeks, so why the hell are you doing an illegal procedure?"

"It's not really illegal, she is only a week or two over and…"

Argus finished his thought, "She paid extra."

The doctor nodded. Karen appeared to be horrified.

"It can't survive on its own."

"What do you call this?" Argus held up the tiny pink girl who was literally fighting for her life with every breath. "She could be saved. Put her on a respirator."

"It's too late for that. She won't survive the hour."

Argus clenched his teeth. Even through his sunglasses, Merrill could see that his eyes were blazing fury, but he recognized dying. Argus knew the doctor was right or he would've rushed out of there to the nearest emergency room. There was nothing that he could do to save her, nothing anyone could do.

Argus turned to Karen, "Get me a glass of water."

"She wouldn't be able to drink the water. It wouldn't do her any good."

"It's not for drinking." Karen did as he asked. Argus took the cup of water as he gently held the tiny fetus in his hand and he poured it over her head.

"I baptize you in the name of the Father and the Son, and the Holy Spirit. Amen."

The doctor went to say something about the pointlessness, not to mention the fact he didn't know that if the mother was Catholic, but one look at Argus' face persuaded him to keep his opinions silent.

"Everybody out."

"We have patients scheduled."

"Out."

"What if they make the attempt while you are in here?"

"Then you die and I give your widow a refund."

The doctor was wrong. The young girl lasted almost an hour and a half before she closed her tiny eyes and her heart beat no more. Argus laid her tenderly down on a countertop near the sinks, wrapped her in linens and sterile cloth. He walked out into the hall and motioned for Karen.

"Stay with the body. Don't let anyone touch it until I come back." Karen was hesitant. Then Argus said something he rarely said, "Please."

Karen went and sat with the tiny corpse. Argus stormed out through the waiting room, past Dr. Merrill and out the front door. A quick look up told him everything he needed to know, the barest glint from a pair of eyeglasses on a rooftop. Argus strolled diagonally across the street, away from where he wanted to be. The protestors wisely chose to pretend he wasn't there. Argus walked behind the building opposite the clinic, using a back door stairwell to reach the roof. With skill born of years of practice, he opened the access door without making a sound. A tall thin man, his hair parted to the side, wearing horn-rimmed glasses was peeking up over the edge of the roof. He was waiting and cradling a rifle in his arms. Argus quietly walked up to him and put a bullet in his head. The puff of the silencer came too late to warn the sniper of his impending doom. The man never knew what happened, which as far as Argus was concerned was an act of mercy.

The hitman returned to the clinic. Dr. Merrill blocked his way in the corridor outside the exam rooms.

"Where'd you go? What happened?"

"Your problem is taken care of."

Merrill's eyes went wide and a huge smile came across his face. "Thank you."

Argus grabbed the doctor by his tie, forcibly dragging him

into an empty exam room and shutting the door.

"You will never perform an abortion on any mother whose child is old enough to survive on its own if it gets the proper medical attention. If you do, you will be getting the bullet with your name on it back. I plan to stop in here periodically and wander back into your operating room unannounced in order to make sure this never happens again. Do I make myself understood?"

By this time, Argus had pulled his tie up so high that Merrill was standing on his toes so he didn't get strangled.

"Yes."

Argus dropped the tie and the doctor almost fell to the floor, barely catching himself in time. Without another word, Argus turned and walked out of the room and back to the operating table. He picked up his bag full of cash and the tiny corpse.

"Thank you."

Karen nodded. "What are you going to do with her?"

"When I baptized her, I named her Isabella after my mother. I'm going to provide her with a decent burial."

"What happened here today doesn't usually happen. It was an abomination."

"I know." Argus turned to leave.

Before he got out the door, Karen called to him. "Wait." Argus turned back. "When you arrange the service, could you let me know? I'd like to be there."

Argus nodded. "That would be nice. Thanks."

As Karen watched, she saw him wipe something from his eye as he turned from her. Before she realized what was happening, he was gone.

SMALL SCALE WAR

Todd was nervous but his fury gave him strength. Twelve-year-old boys were often plagued with strong, conflicting emotions and the form in which they appeared was often determined by something as inconsequential as which way the wind was blowing that day.

On that day there was a chill on the breeze.

Todd's spirit had been crushed, trampled, and beaten down into a crippled little wisp, barely as tangible as smoke. The force of his fury was slowly forging what remained of that spirit into a dark and twisted thing.

Todd had never wondered why his Brooklyn neighborhood was virtually crime free. He had always accepted that there were certain men who also shared his neighborhood who made sure nobody defecated where *they* lived. School was a different matter, a place far off the protective barrier that kept the rest of the streets safe.

As a broken spirit with little to lose, Todd made a life altering decision to take things into his own hands. Since his hands alone weren't up to the task he had decided to even the odds with a piece of hardware.

His courage bolstered by visions of his enemys' bodies exploding in bloody pain, Todd slowly stepped into the alleyway. At the end of the dead end, a man stood waiting, although the title of man might have been a trifle premature. Anton, at seventeen, was only five years older than Todd himself, but he had gotten together his own crew. They handled mostly penny-ante stuff that they were careful to keep outside of the neighborhood. Anton had also dated Todd's sister Rosa for a few months last year. Todd had 'borrowed' his sister's phone to call Anton and had arranged to buy what he needed. Armed with a hundred dollars, Todd entered the alley hoping to walk out armed with something much more deadly.

"Hey Toad," said Anton.

"It's not toad, it's Todd," he said, annoyed at the nickname, a bastardization of his own name. It was something he hated but had become so commonplace at school that he had learned to live with it, although far from happily.

Anton smiled. "No problem. You got the cash?"

Todd nodded. "You got the gun?"

Anton pulled a folded towel out of the inside of his jacket and unwrapped a corner. A gun barrel stuck out. "Was there any doubt?"

Todd looked at the pistol and smiled. Gently his hands reached out almost caressing the weapon. He cradled it gently in his hands.

Todd had never really used a gun before, but he had seen enough TV shows and movies. Convinced it would be easy he tried to take it apart to check it, but was surprised that it was harder than it looked.

Anton took back the gun. "Here, let me show you how to do that."

The older boy showed him how to open it, close it, and dry fire it.

A major deficiency struck Todd. "Where are the bullets?"

Anton shrugged. "You wanted to buy a gun. You didn't say nothing about no bullets."

"I can't use this without bullets."

"You can always buy some bullets on your own."

"I'm twelve freaking years old. No one's going to sell me any bullets in a store. That's why I came to you. If you can't handle it, I'll take my money and go elsewhere." Todd was angry, angry enough that even he didn't know if he was bluffing.

Anton nodded his head in resignation. "I got it with six bullets. I can give you those, beyond that you're on your own. Do we have a deal?"

Todd nodded and held out a hundred dollars. Anton held out

the gun. Each reached for what they wanted, but neither let go of what they were offering.

"The bullets," demanded Todd.

Anton let go of the gun, then pulled open the inside of Todd's jacket and dropped six cartridges into the inside pocket. "Don't even think about taking those out until you are far away from here. That ain't my only gun." Trust was not Anton's strong suit. Todd nodded and let go of the money.

"A pleasure doing business with ya. You need anything else just let me know."

"This should be all that I need," Todd said, tucking the gun in the back of his waistband as he walked out of the alley, bumping straight into a man with dark sunglasses and a black trench coat.

"Argus…" Todd stammered taking a step back.

The man spoke calmly and quietly, in icy tones. "Todd, what are you doing buying a gun?"

"A gun? What are you talking about?" Todd said taking a step back, his hands unconsciously reaching behind him.

"Don't think that being from the neighborhood is going to save me from popping you if you even dare think of pulling a gun on me." Argus had no weapon visible, but Todd couldn't have been more frightened if a stranger had an automatic pointed between his eyes.

Todd put his hands back down to his sides in slow motion.

"Turn around." Todd did as he was instructed and Argus deftly removed the gun from the waistband and then spun the boy back around. "This isn't a gun, it's a piece of crap. It's as likely to blow up in your hand as it is to hurt somebody else. Where'd you get it?"

Todd was frightened and torn. He knew the code as well as anyone – you didn't squeal no matter what. A squealer was the lowest thing on the food chain, but this was Argus. Everybody, even the knockaround guys, were afraid of Argus. Anton would be mad, but Todd didn't even want to imagine what Argus might do to him.

Before Todd could answer, Anton appeared around the curve at the back of the alley. Seeing Argus, he froze.

"Ah," Argus said, getting the answer to his question. "Todd, you don't move until I come back." There was no 'or else'. There didn't need to be.

Argus walked into the alley and Anton sprinted the other way, momentarily forgetting that it was a dead end. As soon as he realized he was trapped, he began banging on doors, begging for someone to let him in. It took seconds for Argus to catch up to him.

From the open end where Todd was doing his best imitation of a statue, he could hear Anton begging and pleading until his cries transformed into blood-curdling screams, then nothing. Dead silence.

Argus emerged alone and returned to where Todd was waiting. Argus took the gun that had been at the heart of this transaction and broke it down to its component parts and dropped each one into a nearby drainage grate. When the last piece was sinking into the sewer, Argus handed Todd back his money.

"Is Anton dead?"

Argus shook his head. "Had to make sure he wouldn't try to pull that crap again. He's passed out with just a broken leg. Being from the neighborhood brought him that much mercy. Let's see what it gets you. What do you need the gun for?"

Todd thought about lying, making something up, but then Argus pulled his sunglasses down to the end of his nose. Argus looked at him and it was as if he was a deer caught in headlights – dark, cold headlights that seemed to rip right through his soul. All thoughts of lying flew from his head.

"For these guys at school who keep bullying me. I was going to make them stop."

"With a gun? Why not just fight back?" asked Argus.

"I tried. There's three of them. They're all bigger than I am. Every time I fought back it got worse. Last week they pissed on me and stole my clothes. I had to go home in my underwear."

"I know that it might be considered a radical thought, but have you tried telling the principal and your parents?" asked Argus.

"Yes, but it didn't make a difference. One of the boys is Jimmy

Rossa."

"Vinnie the Rose's son," answered Argus.

Todd nodded. "Even the principal is afraid of his father. Jimmy gets to do whatever the hell he wants because no one is going to go up against Vinny's kid. I'd almost be willing to sell my soul to get even with him," Todd said.

For a moment, Argus' expression softened. "Trust me, kid, I've been down that road and it's nothing but pain. Someone named Nick offers, you say no, no matter how good it sounds. Besides, you start shooting kids and your soul would end up in the same place anyway. Killing is not the answer."

"But that's what you do," Todd said, before he could catch himself.

"Killing is only a solution, it's never the answer. Maybe we can fix your problem without the bloodshed."

Todd's face lit up. "You mean you'll help me?"

Argus reached over and plucked back the money he had returned to the kid. "Sure. We'll call this your down payment."

Todd had a guilty look creep across his face.

"What?" asked Argus.

"I kinda stole the money from my Mom's pocketbook," Todd admitted.

"Not my problem. That's between you and her. This is between you and me."

Argus reached into Todd's inside jacket pocket and removed the six cartridges. He dropped five of them into the nearby sewer grate. Then he removed a pen-like engraving tool from his own pocket and scribbled something on the bullet.

"What are you doing?" asked Todd.

"You've heard how I do business. I have certain rules. They're very simple. We go under the assumption that you are being truthful and forthcoming about everything that you have told me. As a matter of fact, you are going to swear to me on this bullet on which I have carved your name. If it turns out that anything that you have told me is wrong or not true, this bullet will be how I settle up with you." Todd's face turned ashen. "Anything you want to change or add to your story?"

"No," Todd rasped, shaking and trembling.

Argus held his hand out and Todd placed his own over the bullet.

"Do it."

"I swear on this bullet that everything that I have told you is the truth."

Argus added. "And I understand the consequences if I'm lying."

Todd repeated it.

"Good." Argus put the bullet in his front pocket. "It's been awhile since I've gone to school. Do you think I'll need a hall pass?"

"No. Absolutely not. I absolutely forbid you to be anywhere near my school," said James Pepper, the principal of Todd's high school.

"I don't think that you are exactly in a position to forbid me to do anything," Argus said, leaning back in the principal's own chair which he had commandeered as soon as he walked into the office. He placed his booted feet up onto the principal's desk.

"I won't allow someone with guns in my school. These students are my responsibility," Pepper said. "If you don't leave, I'll be forced to call the police."

"You could do that," conceded Argus. "But then I'd be forced to tell them how I stopped one of your students from putting bullet holes into several of your other students because you failed to stop him from being bullied."

"What!? I would never allow something like that to happen."

"Really? That's not what I hear. The bullies in question are Jimmy Rossa and his friends."

All color drained from the principal's face, almost as if someone had quickly cut his jugular.

"That shut you up. Why haven't you done anything to put a stop to it?"

"Well, we have received a couple of... unconfirmed reports of problems, but I spoke to Jimmy..."

"Who threw his daddy in your face."

The principal shrugged. "I had Mr. Rossa come in for a parent conference to explain the problem…"

"And Vinny gave you some line about boys will be boys and then told you to leave his son alone. Hell, if Vinny is true to form he also managed to get you the raise the boy's grades."

The principal's posture made him appear to shrink in on himself. "Maybe we found a little extra credit for Jimmy to help him out…"

"Your lack of balls almost got Jimmy and his friends dead, not to mention who knows how many innocents. It would be much more fun dealing with the Rossas after that, wouldn't it? Not to mention the Board of Education inquiry board, the news media, and a hell of a lot of angry parents. The sad thing is the threat's probably not over. These boys are crossing the line between bullying and torturing their victims. I've been hired by one of the victims to take care of them."

Argus didn't think the principal could get any paler but he did. "You mean that you are going to…"

"Hardly. Just going to teach those boys a lesson they aren't apparently going to learn in your school. And you're going to help me."

Argus spent most of the morning investigating things on his own, questioning bullying victims. By the time lunch was ready to roll around he had a pretty good idea that Todd's story was absolutely true. Argus went into the boys' bathroom on the first floor, where most of the attacks had taken place. He made himself comfortable in the stall on the far end and waited.

It didn't take long. Apparently, fear wasn't enough to keep some kids from answering the call of nature. The victims were working together. One braved the restroom first, looking under all of the stalls. Argus had his feet up and went unnoticed. Figuring that it was empty he signaled his friends in the hall and the lot of pimply faced teens rushed in to relieve their bladders.

Jimmy Rossa and his two friends were smarter and had been outside watching. Once the five boys were using the urinals they walked in. One of the boys was so frightened that he turned, covering his neighbor's leg in urine.

Jimmy and one of his pals, a football player judging by his bulk, walked towards their version of an ATM machine while the other crony guarded the door.

"Who wants to donate first?" Jimmy asked.

Two boys without a sound zipped up their pants and handed money to the football goon. The goon acting as doorman let the pair leave untouched.

The third boy wasn't so lucky. He started backing away to the rear of the bathroom.

"What's the matter? You don't have your payment?" asked Gene, the football player.

The boy was shaking.

"You took my lunch money on Monday. You made me give you my allowance on Tuesday."

"Yeah, but today is Wednesday."

"I don't have any more money."

Jimmy shrugged. "Then you should've borrowed or stole some. Now I'm going to get creative on your ass. Drop your pants."

Realizing what was about to happen, the boy screamed, "No, please don't."

"Pull 'em down to your ankles now."

"No," said the boy, defiant and ready to fight.

"You sound like you have a choice. Bend over, Billy…" Jimmy unzipped his own pants.

The football goon moved forward to the weaker boy. As he came close to the stall door, Argus stepped out and grabbed him by the hair and slammed his face into the wall. The football goon slid to the floor as quietly and silently as an old nightmare.

"Who the hell are you?"

Argus didn't answer, but took a step putting himself between the boy and Jimmy.

"We're going to hurt you. No one messes with me. Joey, hurt him."

The goon from the door moved forward relatively unafraid.

Before he could take a swing at Argus, the hit man slashed out with his boot to the inside of his left knee followed quickly by a punch to the throat. He fell to the floor gasping for air. Argus snap kicked him once in the jaw and he was unconscious.

"You just made the biggest mistake of your life. Do you know who I am?"

"Yeah, you're a punk kid leaning on his father's rep."

"My father's rep is going to kill your ass."

"Not gonna happen. Since were playing the name game, do you know who I am?"

"No, and soon it won't matter who you were. Don't matter who a corpse was."

"Very scary. I guess that works on kids, but you're not dealing with a kid now, Jimmy. Do you know who the Soul for Hire is?"

"Yeah. Vince Argus, the best freaking hit man who ever lived. Now you're probably going to claim you're friends with him, I'd guess? Well, you know what? I am going to have my Dad hire him to kill you."

"I doubt that very much."

"Why? You think that you're too close for Argus to take a hit on you? He'll do it because he'll want to make my father happy and because no one turns down money. Anyone can be bought."

"Maybe not everybody. And for the record, the Soul for Hire and I are close. As a matter of fact, we're like this," Argus said, holding up a single index finger. "And I ain't going to shoot myself on your say so."

Jimmy's jaw dropped and he took a step back, truly scared for the first time in his whole young life. "You're Argus?"

In answer, Argus's lips briefly turned upward in a shadow of a smile.

"Shit."

"So, you've changed your tune have ya, Jimmy boy? I think that you should give this gentleman back his money." The boy in question had backed up into the corner, trying to remain silent and as still as possible in hopes that his presence would go unnoticed. The other two victims were trying the same tact.

"You want me to give him his money back?" Argus nodded. Jimmy grinned. "Sure, no problem." He tossed some bills into a urinal that hadn't been flushed from several uses. "He wants his money he can go in and get it."

Argus didn't speak. He replied with his actions. Grabbing Jimmy by the back of his collar he slammed his forehead into the top of the urinal and pushed down with such force that Jimmy fell to his knees and had his face slammed into the yellow water.

Argus held him there for the better part of a minute. When he yanked his head up Jimmy was gasping for air. Before he could get a decent breath of air, Argus did it again.

The next time his head was above the urine line, Jimmy yelled, "Stop! I'll give him his money back."

"Yeah you are, but first get that out from where you put it."

Jimmy reached his hand up towards the bowl, but Argus slapped it away.

"Oh no, you are going to have to get that with your teeth."

"Oh hell no." Argus again slammed his face into the urinal. Blood was trickling from his lips and his nose and a huge welt had formed on his forehead. "Either you start bobbing for bills or the Rose isn't going to be able to recognize his own son." Jimmy reluctantly complied, throwing up his twice before the bills were out.

"Now give him some clean bills."

Jimmy did as he was told.

"Very good. Time to feel a little of what you've been dishing out. Strip down."

"No way."

"Do it or I am going to hurt you."

"You already hurt me," said Jimmy.

"Boy, that's nothing but a bunch of love taps. If I hurt you, you're going to know it and feel it for the rest of your days. Now either you are naked as a pole dancer by the time I count to ten or else you're not going to be able to walk out of here. One…"

Jimmy had started stripping.

"That goes for all three of you."

"But Gene is still knocked out."

"Don't care. Take his clothes off of him yourselves and then the lot of you carry him out."

The boys followed the instructions glowering the whole time.

"Now get out of here," Argus said.

"I'm going to tell my dad," Jimmy said.

"Good. Tell him I'll be there to see him in an hour."

"What about our clothes?"

"That's the least of your worries. Get out."

The three youths left at a fast pace carrying their unconscious friend.

"Now you three make sure that you tell nobody about what Jimmy tried to do, but you can tell everybody about the rest of what happened here, understand?"

"Yes sir," the boys replied in unison.

As they left, Argus stopped and contemplated the urinals. "Seemed higher when I was in school."

Vinnie the Rose was not happy. In less than an hour, he'd gotten every knockaround guy he could get a hold of and they were waiting in Vito's. Jimmy had changed some of the details of the story to make himself look better so his father was letting paternal concern and anger get the better of him. Argus knew this would be the case and he wanted to diffuse the situation.

The Rose sat in the center of the room, almost totally still while everyone around him paced.

The Rose picked his ringing cell phone out of his jacket pocket, looking at it. Very few people had that number and even fewer of them were encouraged to use it. Ever.

He flipped the top open. "This is Vinny… Argus! What the frig did you do to my kid!? I don't care how good you are no one does this…" Vinny listened and got awful quiet. "All right, fine, but get your ass in here." The Rose slammed down the phone. "Everyone put away your guns."

This got him confused and perturbed looks.

"Which one of you wants to try and start a gun fight with Argus?" The men reluctantly put away their weapons.

"Course that doesn't mean we can't have any insurance. Johnny, go hide in the coat check room, just in case."

Argus walked in the door, ever present sunglasses covering his eyes. Barely a step in, he pulled two automatics from under his leather trench coat and used one to shoot through the wall of the coat room. Johnny screamed as his hand exploded and his gun hit the floor. One of the knockaround guys on the other side of the room started to reach for his gun, but Argus drew with his other hand faster. He put a bullet through the man's palm before his hand could clear the holster. Argus then trained the two weapons loosely around the room.

"Vinnie, I called you to avoid this kind of crap. First off, if you're going to have someone hide in the coat room make sure the guy walking in the door can't see the reflection in the mirror. Second, if any of you try to draw on me again the next bullet is not going to be so kindly placed. Now would you people take care of your bleeding friends? And if anyone else is stupid enough to try anything, you're going to need some body bags."

Argus walked over to the Rose's table and sat down. He didn't get too relaxed and his hands still held his weapons.

"Are you going to put those away?" asked the Rose.

"No."

"That doesn't show good manners or trust."

"It does show a hell of a lot of intelligence. Vinnie, you just tried to ambush me. I'd be within my rights to put a bullet through your skull, but because of our past I'm not going to do that." Argus got a big grin on his face. "At least not yet. Why don't we just get down to business?"

"Fine. Do you want to explain to me why you beat up my kid and sent him home naked through the neighborhood?" demanded the Rose.

"Simple. I was saving his life."

It was the last answer the Rose expected to hear. "You want to explain that?"

"Be happy to. Your son and two of his associates were running a little bit of a shake down ring at the school."

Vinnie beamed proudly at the revelation. "Nothing wrong with that. He's following in his old man's footsteps I used to do the same."

"I remember. The problem is, young Jimmy was doing things his dad never did."

"Such as?"

"For one thing, he was pissing and defecating on some of his victims."

That got a bunch of laughs around the room. Vinnie just shrugged with a half-smile. "Boys will be boys. Sometimes they get a little carried away."

"One of his victims was going to go Columbine on his ass. If I hadn't done this, he'd have a bullet in his head right now."

Vinny moved his head from side to side in contemplation. "For that I can thank you, but for how you did it there's got to be some reckoning."

"We'll see if you feel that way once you find out the rest."

"I'm waiting."

Argus looked around the room. "I feel it would be something best spoken of in private."

"You can tell me here."

"No, I can't. Trust me." To prove his point, Argus demonstrated trust and put away his guns. "Perhaps you and I in your office?"

Vinnie nodded. "Vito, get us a bottle of Chianti and two glasses."

"I'll go in too," said Jimmy.

"You'll wait here," Vinnie the Rose said in a tone that would brook no argument.

Vito delivered the bottle on the desk in the office and left. Argus went in, followed closely by Vinnie who closed the door behind them.

Vinnie poured them each a glass and they toasted each other. "Salute."

"Argus, why would you do what you did to Jimmy?"

"I told you part of it."

"Saving his life."

"Yes. But there was more. He disrespected me and you."

"How did he do this?"

"First, he threatened my life."

"Jimmy threatened you!?"

"He did not realize who I was, but he used your name as if he spoke for you. He told me he would tell you to have me killed. I assume you do not allow your son to speak in your voice."

"No. Jimmy knows better."

"No, he does not. He did it several times. I got the impression he makes a habit of doing it to the other students, teachers, and the principal. He even said he would hire *me* to do the killing before I told him who I was. You know *I* do not allow anyone to speak in my voice. He said I could be bought, made to do anything he wanted, paid for by your money. It was an insult to my honor. That alone justified my actions. Then when I told him who I was, there was no apology. Instead the threats continued and he vowed again that you would have me killed. For me to have done any less to him would have been a sign of weakness on my honor. I will not do that for anyone, not even you."

"I apologize for my son. I will make this right, but you will have to make right what you did as well."

"I already have. I saved his life, did him no permanent bodily harm for his disrespect and protected your honor."

"Argus, what are you taking about?"

"Jimmy was about to go a little *fenucca*. I stopping him from raping a boy, a child who could not pay, in front of other children. Had I not stopped him, word would have leaked out." Argus did not have to say what damage it would do to the Rose's honor if word got out. In Vinnie's world, homosexuality was considered a great weakness. Men had been killed for nothing less than being found out to have had an affair with another man. For the Rose's son to be known as gay would not only shame Vinnie, but be seen as a sign of weakness which would lead to tests of his power, if not outright rebellion.

"Argus, are you sure? Could you be mistaken?"

"No," Argus said.

The Rose did not move or blink for a long time. When he did, he uncoiled like a violent spring throwing the bottle of Chianti so hard it shattered on the wall.

Vito opened the door. "Vinnie, you okay?" There was no gun drawn but that could have changed in a moment.

"Get Jimmy in here now!"

"Yes, boss."

The son of the Rose was hustled into the office and the door quietly shut behind him.

"So, Dad, did he apologize..."

"Sit and shut up," shouted Vinnie.

Jimmy started to speak but thought better of it. Instead, he glared at Argus who was now leaning against a wall, his face set like a statue.

"You know never to threaten someone as if you are speaking for me."

"I wouldn't..." Jimmy's response was answered by a backhanded slap to the face.

"I told you to shut up. Then you threatened Argus who has been a friend to this family."

"He's lying." Answered with another slap.

"I owe Argus my life from a time before you were born, which means you owe him yours. Argus could easily have killed you and made you disappear with no one being the wiser. It would have been much easier than risking a war with us, but he didn't. By calling him a liar you insult his honor. If he is lying, there will be war. If he's not, you have insulted his honor. Tell me the truth – is he lying or not?"

"Of course, he's..."

"Jimmy, your father's not a dumb man. If there is a conflict between our stories, he's going to interview everyone who was there, the victims and your crew. You won't be present. What do you think your boys will say alone in a back room with Vito and the boys, let alone your victims? Of course, then your actions become public and even your father won't be able to protect you then. Think about that before your answer."

Jimmy's glare at Argus was full of hate and fury, but he looked down and whispered, "He's not lying."

"I was proud when I heard what you and your crew were doing. I never involved you in my business, but was pleased when you went into it on your own. I would never have allowed adults to work that school, but you are my son so I turned a blind eye. Business is business after all, but business has rules. You knew them, yet you broke them. That is unacceptable from anyone, especially my own son. For you to try to rape a boy, that is so wrong. I have never been more ashamed in my life. If you were not my son, you'd be dead now."

"Dad, it's no big deal. I was teaching him a lesson."

The Rose's face went dark. He stood up and yanked his son up out of his chair and smashed his face with his palm so hard that it sent him to the ground.

Jimmy screamed as he held his hands up to ward off his father's blows, but his father kept hitting.

Finally, exhausted, the Rose stopped, his son bloody and bleeding.

"Argus, I'll make this right."

Argus nodded and left the office and the bar.

There was a knock on the apartment door and Jennie opened it with the safety chain still on. She got very nervous when she saw who it was.

"Yes?'

"Mrs. Franco, I need to speak with Todd," Argus said in a very polite and respectful tone.

"What's he done?"

"Nothing. He hired me and I wanted to update him on the job."

"He hired you?" The implication hung in the air. "He wouldn't..."

"Please let me in. I'm sure this isn't something you want broadcast in the hallway, nosy neighbors and all."

Trembling, Jennie shut the door and took the chain off, and let Argus in. "Todd, come in here."

"What? I'm busy," Todd shouted from his room.

"Your mother said get in here. You should respect and listen to her," Argus said.

Hearing the voice, Todd ran into the living room.

"Mr. Argus says you hired him? Why and how would you do that?" Jennie asked.

"Remember the bullies at school?"

Jennie put her hand over her mouth. "Oh my God!"

"Don't worry Mrs. Franco, nobody died. I just wanted to let Todd know he won't be having any problems anymore."

"I heard about what happened, but when Jimmy comes back he'll be pissed..."

"Jimmy won't be coming back." Jennie's eyes opened wide and she gasped. "His father is sending him away to private school."

"Thank you," Todd said.

"You're welcome. Thank you for your time, Mrs. Franco. I'll show myself to the door."

As Argus left, he could hear Todd's mother yelling at him, asking about the hows and the whys of what happened. Argus briefly cracked a smile before his face shifted back to the stone mask that he kept between himself and the rest of the world.

A BULLET
FOR THE DEAD

Vince Argus had never charged by the hour. When people hired a hitman, they expected a set price. People felt uncomfortable and intimidated arguing expenses with a professional killer. Argus charged on a sliding scale, based on the client's finances and the misdeeds of the target. It had worked well up until now, but after having tried to eliminate Jacob McMillian, he was considering revising that policy.

It started easily enough. McMillian was a low-level loan shark who was not associated with any larger organization. Shirley Darling had hired the hitman to avenge her husband. Her dearly departed mate had been into McMillian for one grand and the shark had murdered him for missing a single payment. It was, on the surface, an unusual business decision. Killing someone means they won't be able to pay what they owe, which is why leg and finger breaking was so popular in that business.

In this case, the purpose wasn't to teach Darling a lesson so much as to educate a bigger fish who owed him a hundred and fifty large and who was thinking about missing a payment. Darling's battered and beaten corpse was left on that man's front porch, with pieces missing that were never to be found.

The bigger fish hadn't missed a payment since and Darling's grand was written off as business expenses. Which was no comfort to the Widow Darling and their two little Darlings, left without a father. The cops had nothing to go on but their suspicions and that wasn't even enough to bring McMillian in for questioning.

"I need him to die," the Widow Darling growled between tears.

Argus nodded and handed her an engraved bullet.

"Why is my name carved on this?" she asked, her mind's protective instincts overcoming her heart's need for vengeance.

Argus smiled. It didn't give the Widow Darling any comfort at all, nor was it meant to. She did find herself being grateful for the dark shades that covered the hitman's eyes because as angry as she was, she didn't think she could gaze into those murky orbs and still speak coherently.

"I live by a code and others die by it, but some are exempted. No innocents. No family. No children. People willing to end someone's life, especially those seeking to do it by proxy, tend to be looking out for themselves instead of me. Clients have been known to lie, to fabricate entire stories to get what they want. I'm not someone who appreciates being toyed with or lied to. I find this custom cuts down on problems."

"Custom?" asked the Widow Darling.

"For me to kill this man for you, you must first swear on this bullet. If I find that you have lied or misled me in any way, that bullet will be coming back for you out of the barrel of my gun."

The Widow Darling swallowed and her saliva, as startled by this revelation as the rest of her, went down the wrong pipe and started a coughing fit. Argus sat silent and unmoving until she stopped.

"Still want to hire me?" he asked.

The Widow Darling nodded, meekly at first, then stronger. "McMillian killed my husband. Hell, yes, I want you to kill him." She held the bullet in the palm of her hand. "I swear everything I have told you is true."

Argus reached out to retrieve the bullet, brushing the skin of the widow's palm. The touch startled her and caused her to shiver involuntarily before freezing, afraid she might have offended the killer.

Argus noticed but paid it no mind. He had long ago given up trying to interact with his clients as anything more than a Soul for Hire.

"How much do you want?" asked the widow. "Buddy had a life insurance policy, but I had hoped to save at least some of that for the girls' college."

Argus had checked. Buddy Darling had fifty thousand in

insurance and twenty in debt. Argus had more money than he needed, so he wasn't above mercy in his pricing. He felt for the woman who had lost her husband. Argus knew the pain of losing loved ones to a killer intimately, and despite his fearsome reputation, he did have a heart.

"One thousand."

"That's all? I thought…"

"His life was taken for that much. It's appropriate his killer's is taken for the same."

"Thank you," the widow said, bowing her head and kissing his hand. She had seen one too many movies, but Argus let it go. He found following imagined customs helped clients cope with a difficult situation.

Argus simply nodded and left. Unfortunately, there was one important thing the Widow Darling had left out, but it wasn't her fault. Shirley Darling didn't know that Jacob McMillian was already dead.

Argus did his usual recon of the target. McMillian didn't bother much with bodyguards or vests. He barely bothered looking up and down a street before he left a building. It was too easy.

City born and breed, the Soul for Hire didn't know much about looking gift horses in the mouth, but if he did, he was the type who would be checking for plastic explosives disguised as teeth.

Because it looked so simple, he did extra surveillance, but McMillian was still as sloppy with personal security on day five as he was on day one.

Day six was when Argus took the shot. As a hitman, he obviously did sniper work. With the marksmanship gifts the Devil had given him in exchange for his soul, it was child's play. Within the physical specs of a weapon's force and range, he literally couldn't miss. It didn't mean the target couldn't shift or something couldn't suddenly block the bullet's path, but Argus was a professional and accounted for that.

Still, he did not take a life, even that of another killer, lightly. Whenever feasible, he tried to do the deed up-close and personal.

It was one of the few times he took off his sunglasses. At the moment of death, even a scumbag deserved the respect of being looked in the eyes by the man who killed him. Of course, his safety and continued freedom often dictated a different approach, but McMillian seemed like a cakewalk.

Of course, strolling on a cake big enough to walk across would be akin to walking through a swamp filled with sticky sweet quicksand.

Argus stepped out of an alley, his gun already pointed at McMillian's face. He waited until their gazes met, and then put a bullet between the big man's eyes. McMillian's cranium did the familiar snap back and the big man hit the pavement. Argus knew the damage a bullet could do at point blank range when it went into a skull and there hadn't been enough blood spatter for a head wound. The Soul for Hire mentally wrote it off to low blood pressure. Sure, the big guys tended to have high blood pressure, but there were exceptions to every rule.

Argus left through the alley, planning to disappear out the other side, when another rule was broken. The man who had a bullet rip through his skull got up off the pavement, brushed himself off, and began to play with the wound using his index finger.

Despite his better judgment, Argus stopped his escape to watch. There was no question that he hadn't missed, and the hitman's brain was speeding to re-assess the situation. Bored with fingering his torn flesh, McMillian looked up and noticed the man who had just shot him. He waved with his free hand, smiling with an expression of purest glee. The flesh had already started to mend, so when McMillian took his finger out of the crater in his head, it made a slurpy pop. Not bothering to wipe the brains off his digit, the dead man cracked his knuckles and took a single step toward the Soul for Hire.

Argus was the kind of cool and tough that intimidated other tough guys, but he wasn't stupid. You didn't stay and blindly shoot at something that had already proved that bullets don't hurt it when a perfectly good escape route was available, so he turned and ran. The dead man stopped, choosing to stay put, but the sounds of McMillian's laughter chased the Soul for Hire for hours.

The next day, McMillian didn't change his routine. Apparently, a bullet to the head wasn't enough to make him vary anything. For Argus, it was enough to make him change his game plan. From a nearby roof, he used a combination of armor piercing and exploding rounds to turn the dead man's entire torso and head into the consistency of hamburger and Swiss cheese.

Argus disdained flash. It attracted too much attention. A bullet in a darkened area showed up on page seven of the newspapers or twenty minutes into the local broadcast news. A hit in front of a crowd was front-page headlines and the lead on the evening news. Quiet was always preferable, just not always possible. Sometimes it was because the target's security was too good. In this case, it was because getting too close to the target again seemed foolhardy.

McMillian's corpse lay still and unmoving. Argus allowed himself a rare smile but didn't move. It was too important to make sure the target stayed dead, and he had called in a phony tip that would have the police busy elsewhere. He estimated he had at least four more minutes before he had to vacate.

Most people had taken cover or wisely run away, but some had started to venture out and block his view of the corpse goo, but even as far away as he was, he knew there was less of it spread around the street than there had been earlier.

"Damn it," he swore under his breath, as the head reformed and the gelatinous eyes became whole and glared up at him. McMillian wasn't laughing now. Argus left a full three minutes before police arrived, which was thirty seconds after McMillian was whole enough to scoop up the remaining parts of his scattered and pureed flesh and limp off. The bits and pieces that he missed crawled off after him. By the time the crime scene unit arrived, the blood spatter itself had disappeared, each droplet pilling up into microscopic beads and following the wandering flesh of the fleeing dead man, leaving many unanswered questions about where the evidence of the alleged shooting went.

On day eight, Argus waited for him at a more deserted spot.

The hitman stepped out from behind a dumpster. McMillian stopped and stared.

"Come to apologize?" the dead man asked.

"Nope."

"Then you've come to die." McMillian cracked his knuckles.

"That's not in the cards, either. I want to know why you're still walking around. You make a deal with the Devil?"

McMillian laughed. "The Devil's not real. And if he was, who'd be stupid enough to sell him their soul?"

Argus didn't say a word about someone doing it while covered in the blood, brains, and guts of those he loved most in the world in order to gain revenge on those who had just slaughtered them. This wasn't about Argus.

"You made a deal with something," he said. "If not the Devil, what?"

McMillian laughed. "Not bad for a hired gun. You're right, but it wasn't something from Hell. It was a little old lady who was a voodoo priestess or something. Her grandson was into me for ten large and had no hope of paying. The old broad made me an offer of immortality in exchange for wiping the kid's slate clean. I figured her for a kook but said if she could do it, I'd consider it. She made me wear some sack around my neck with chicken legs and other crap in it. I put it on, but before I got home figured I'd been had.

"Before I could turn around, her grandkid jumped me with a knife and stabbed me in the chest. Turns out he didn't know about the deal the old broad made for him. The punk ran away and left me bleeding in the gutter. I died, but my blood soaked into that sack of shit I was wearing. It changed me. I woke up as a zombie. Any wound I get heals itself. I was worried about pushing it, thinking the magic might have its limits, but after what you did to me yesterday, I know nothing can kill me. It's great being dead."

Argus stared at the dead man's shirt, which made McMillian

grin. "Nice try, but I don't need that voodoo shit anymore. It did its job." The zombie took a step forward and Argus took two back. "And don't waste your time trying to find the old bitch to ask her for a way to kill me. When I rose up I went looking for her grandson, but he had gone to ground. I looked at grandma's, but he wasn't there.

"But she was. And I realized if she gave me this power, she could take it away. I snuck in the back and snapped her neck like a twig. And made a little snack of her, but she was mostly gristle. That's the one drawback of being a zombie—the damn hunger for human flesh, but I can live with that. Or not live with it, as is the case."

McMillian cracked his knuckles. "You're stupider than you look if you think you're gonna get a chance at bat for strike three."

Argus held his hands up to show they were empty. "This time, I just came to talk."

The dead man shrugged. "Sorry. Don't believe you. And even if I did, I need a snack. Regenerating all that flesh from when you shot me up yesterday made me real hungry. I can't be killed, but the cops can still lock me up. True, it'd take a hundred of 'em, but they got more than that. Mmm, should I start with white meat or dark? Maybe a little of both."

"I hate to ruin your dinner plans but I'm not on the menu today. Still, I hate to see you go hungry." Argus reached under his leather trench coat, but instead of pulling out a gun his hand emerged with a piece of rope. McMillian started to smile until he realized that tied to each end was a hand grenade. "I brought pineapple surprise." Before he had finished speaking, Argus had pulled the pins and threw the homemade bolo so it wrapped around the zombie's neck.

"Oh shit," said McMillian when he saw a grenade land near each ear. Argus had already dived to take shelter behind a dumpster.

The explosion turned the dead man's head to mush. Argus pulled out two more grenade bolos, one in each hand. These he threw together. One wrapped around the dead man's torso, the other around his knees.

Even the four explosions that followed weren't enough to do more that turn McMillian's flesh to a meaty mess. Within moments, the body was knitting itself back together.

"Make things right with your maker. Next time we end this," Argus promised, a plan already forming. He hoped he could still find an open hardware store.

Once his body had sewn itself back into a recognizable form, McMillian found himself in an understandably foul mood. Even in life, the dead man had never been one to suffer alone. Finding someone weaker to inflict misery on was, if not a cure for the blues, a wonderful Band-Aid. Now everyone was weaker than he was.

After busting up a bar and fourteen men, five of which he killed outright, McMillian was feeling urges he hadn't felt in a long time. Pounding in some jerk's face had always made him horny as hell, and doing it to more than a dozen guys made his mind remember what usually came next. McMillian wasn't even sure the equipment still worked, but he had some medicinal aids in his pocket that he had been carrying around for just such an occasion.

He visited his favorite cathouse and asked for not one, not even two, but five girls to sate his lusty appetite. The Madame, a lady by the name of Suzie Jane, would have been more than happy to oblige, but first, she explained that it would be five times the fee.

McMillian told her he wasn't even going to pay the regular price, explaining that he had decided to take over the rackets from the mob and anyone else who stood in his way.

As it happened, Suzie Jane already paid protection to the mob and some of the gentlemen liked to take it out in trade. Three of them were present when the dead man started making trouble. The trio were partners, working together as a team to do things even they felt were best left unsaid, but they had rarely had a problem handling just one guy.

Working in sync, they came at the zombie from three angles, knowing he couldn't defend himself from all of them. McMillian didn't even try. As two of the men grabbed his arms, the third slammed a haymaker in the dead man's gut. McMillian didn't even flinch. Instead, he lifted up his arms, and the two men left the ground with the zombie's upper extremities. McMillian slammed their heads together like they were a couple of cymbals. The blow hurt each of them. It wasn't enough to knock them out, but neither was able to hold on. Next, the dead man head-butted the front man's head, sinking his teeth into the mob man's nose. When he pulled back, the man's nose tore away in his teeth.

The man's hand shot up to his face, and he watched as McMillian sucked the nasal meat into his mouth. This was followed by much chewing and a large, swallowing gulp.

The realization that McMillian had just eaten his nose angered the mob man beyond any fury he had ever had before. When McMillian smiled and burped, it would be a fair assessment to say the leg breaker lost it. Pulling out his gun he pumped the entire clip of ten bullets into the zombie's head pan. The force of the wounds knocked the dead man down.

Thinking the nose-eater was dead, the man without a nose knelt over his body and pulled out a knife that could easily have skinned a bear.

One of his companions tried to pull at his shoulder. "We need to get out of here."

The man without a nose slapped the hand away. "Not until I gut him and get my nose back. We'll take it to the doctor to reattach."

"He chewed it pretty good. I don't know if—"

"Shaddup and get me some ice," the man without a nose ordered.

"Suzie Jane, get him lots of ice," the second man delegated.

"What are you going to do about the dead body in my parlor?" the Madame demanded.

"We'll take care of the f'ing body. Get me the goddamned ice," the man with no nose said as his knife sliced into the dead man's stomach, his free hand peeling back flesh to find the stomach.

Which was when McMillian's brain had reformed enough to give him back motor control of his body. The dead man sat up, which had two immediate effects. First, there was much screaming and terror from those who witnessed it, followed by a bit of praying and cursing which decreased as the people doing said vocal activity fled the area.

Unfortunately for the man with no nose, he was stuck fast, his hand trapped between ribs and pelvis as the flesh knitted around his knife hand. Pull as he might, he was stuck as fast as if he had grabbed hold of the mythical tar baby.

"That tickles," McMillian said.

"What the hell are you?" the man with no nose demanded. Blood spurted from the bare nasal cavity to punctuate his words.

"The new order. Sadly, for you, you're my appetizer," McMillian said, trying to twist off the man's head. Even with enhanced strength, a human head does not readily or easily detach from its perch on the spine, so the dead man had to twist it around several times and wiggle it back and forth quite a bit before it finally came off. What McMillian had to do to get at the brain was even worse, and caused the partners of the man with no nose—who had now become the man with no head—to flee in terror, leaving behind several women of questionable repute quite ill and petrified because the dead man was between them and the door so they had no place to run.

Meanwhile, Argus had found out that McMillian had finally decided to vary from his usual routine. Argus managed to track him to the bar but found the survivors of the bar fight were far more afraid of a dead man than a hitman.

However, not everyone was cowed. One of the injured, who was being wheeled on a gurney to a waiting ambulance, recognized the Soul for Hire.

"Argus," he gasped. "You're going after the bastard that did this?"

"Yes."

"He mentioned going to Suzie Jane's."

"Thanks," said Argus.

"Blow his nuts off," the man said.

"McMillian's not getting off that easy," Argus promised, going outside and around the corner to a waiting unmarked motorcycle.

He donned a black helmet and flipped down its tinted visor. To take out McMillian, he was going to have to resort to a minor amount of flash, and it was best no one recognized him.

Argus arrived at Suzie Jane's in time to see the mass exodus of screaming prostitutes and johns. He drove right through the front door and into the parlor. McMillian turned in time to see the motorcycle, but Argus didn't even slow down. His Hell-bought reflexes worked as well with a bike as they did with a gun and he raced around the zombie, tying a metal cable around his neck and torso. McMillian reached to try to pull the steel bindings off, but the motion was stopped short by the motorcycle speedily exiting the premises. The cable followed the bike and McMillian was yanked off his feet and dragged behind it.

Argus didn't slow below eighty and reached speeds of 120 MPH as he raced through the dark city streets, far too fast for the police to keep up if someone actually took the time to dial 911.

The Soul for Hire swerved and weaved constantly, too fast to allow the zombie to get his bearings but not extreme enough to rip off any body parts that would allow the dead man to escape. When he arrived outside a construction site that was closed for the evening, the hitman revved the bike into high gear and hit the ramp he had set up earlier. The bike soared over the fence and into the walled yard of the site. McMillian hit the ramp and took to the air, but not nearly as gracefully as the motorcycle had.

The sound of the bike drowned out the noise that the gas powered industrial mulcher made, so it was a surprise to McMillian when his neck hit a sharpened blade and decapitated him. His torso landed right at the opening of the mulcher, his head off to the side, neck side down, so his eyes could see.

Anyone looking would have sworn it was an accident. No one was lucky enough to pull that off. Argus would agree. Having the Devil own your soul was the furthest thing from lucky he could think of, except maybe for what was happening to McMillian.

Argus didn't worry about the head when he leapt off the bike. Instead, he flipped a switch to put the mulcher into high gear. The cable slid off now that there was no head to hold it on. Argus lifted the dead man's feet off the ground and pushed him neck first into the flashing blades of the machines, which ground his dead flesh into goo. Argus didn't let go until all he was left holding was a pair of messy shoes.

McMillian's head tried to laugh, but couldn't manage it without lungs or a windpipe.

Argus walked over and stood over the disembodied head.

"You think your body is going to come back to you, don't you?" McMillian couldn't nod but smirked, fire and the promise of death gleaming in his eyes. "Not happening. Let me show you why."

Argus picked up the head by the hair. McMillian tried to bite him, but it wasn't hard to avoid his teeth. Argus held the head over the top of the mulching machine, where McMillian's head was able to see a mixer churning cement that had only the slightest tint of crimson, and the fire in his eyes went out. The promise of death stayed, just switched who it was promised to.

"I doubt your pieces will be able to make it out of there, especially once it hardens. I'll make sure the cement goes to different areas, some even underwater. I doubt you'll ever be able to reform."

Although unable to speak, his mouth could still form the words.

Why?

"Mrs. Darling hired me to avenge her husband. You remember your object lesson and snack?"

McMillian's face registered disbelief as if the housewife could never be the cause of his quasi-demise. His lips started moving again.

How much?

Argus had to fight back a smirk.

"A thousand."

What!? The dead man's face was furious. *You killed me for a lousy grand?*

"No, you killed Darling for a grand. I killed you for his lost life plus a thousand bucks."

Argus placed the head in a box, so McMillian had to watch as the cement poured over him. Unable to have last words, he tried for a last mouthing.

I'll get out, and when I do, I'm coming for you.

"I never took you for an optimist." Cement continued to flood the small box. "You have important decisions to make, quite probably the last ones you'll ever have." McMillian squinted at the Soul for Hire. "Do you close your mouth or leave it open? Is it better to be able to move your tongue or just be totally immobilized? And don't forget your eyes. Would it be preferable to look at the backs of your eyelids for all eternity or have something as hard as a rock pressing up against your pupil instead? Not that you'll have any light either way. I wonder if you'll eventually forget what it looked like."

McMillian tried to yell and got a mouthful of cement for his trouble. Moments later, he decided to close his eyes as he was submerged, but the last thing he saw was burned forever into his mind—Argus standing and looking him directly in the eyes, his sunglasses held at his side.

CIVIC
DUTY

"Mr. Costello, how do you feel about the death penalty?"

Spenser Douglas, the Assistant United States Attorney asked.

"It's a necessary evil," Vince Argus said, playing the part of Jeff Costello. The Soul for Hire used the identity when he wanted to escape from unwanted attention or pretend to be a normal person and it was just his luck that Jeff got called for jury duty.

"So, you feel it acts as a deterrent?" Douglas asked.

"To some."

"Would you have any issues finding a man guilty if he might get the death penalty?"

"If the evidence was strong enough and the crime bad enough, I would not."

"Thank you. The prosecution has no objections to this juror."

George Fallow, the defense attorney rose, in a custom-made suit that cost easily ten times what the civil servant on the other side of the courtroom wore. His client was sporting one that was even more expensive, its color and tie designed to make him look sympathetic to a jury.

"Mr. Costello, do you think everyone accused of a capital crime should get the death penalty?"

The Soul for Hire tried not to smile, considering his day job. "Absolutely not."

"Do you always wear sunglasses, even indoors?" the defense attorney said.

"Usually."

"Why? Medical reason? Migraines?"

"It usually makes other people more comfortable."

"Would you mind removing them?"

"Yes, I would."

"Would you remove them anyway?"

Vince Argus slowly pulled off sunglasses and hung them on the collar of his shirt, then turned his attention to the defense attorney. Despite having defended murderers, rapists, white-collar criminals who ruined hundreds of families, and other scumbags, the defense attorney took a step back at the sight of Vince Argus's eyes looking into his.

Still, he was a professional, not thrown simply because a potential juror looked at him in a disturbing way. "Thank you. You are aware that there are people sent to death row who were later found to be innocent?"

"I am."

"So, if there was any question in your mind about whether or not someone committed a capital crime, do you think they should get the death penalty?"

"Taking a life is a terrible thing. Even the life of someone who may be a killer. I do not think every killer deserves the death penalty."

"Very good. Do you live alone?"

"I do."

"The defense has no objections to this witness."

"Mr. Argus, take your seat in the jury box," said the federal judge in the black robes. Argus put his sunglasses back on and stood up.

"Mr. Argus, I would appreciate you not wearing sunglasses in my courtroom."

Vince Argus nodded and took the sunglasses back off, more than a little amused that he had been picked. The judge had asked him the standard questions before the attorneys started- Did he have any family or friends involved in law enforcement. Argus replied he knew some people, but wouldn't call them friends. He also told them he did not know anyone involved in this trial. But there was a moment of hesitation when the judge asked him if he had any close family members that had been the victim of a violent crime.

Argus' parents and six of his siblings had all been wiped out in front of him. The massacre that killed them ended thirty-six lives in all. Argus took three bullets to the gut and one grazed his head. As he lay dying among the corpses of his family, the Devil rose up and offered him a deal – his soul in exchange for eight years of life – one for each member of his family that died. As an added bonus he'd be gifted with the ability to hit any target within the natural capacity of his chosen weapon. That or he could close his eyes and die and let those he loved most in the world go unavenged. There was really no choice. Vince Argus took the Devil's deal. Argus may have been a seventeen year old kid having dinner with his family when he entered that restaurant, but he left it a Soul for Hire.

But that tragedy happened to Vince Argus, *not* Jeff Costello, so as Jeff he answered no.

It seemed to him that the high-priced defense team had done a sloppy job of getting rid of jurors who might not be sympathetic to their client. It seemed more important to them that the person lived by themselves. And because of the publicity, the defense requested from the start that the jury be sequestered. The judge agreed so the federal government put them up in a nice hotel.

Argus payed rapt attention as both sides presented their cases, fascinated about the inner workings of a murder trial, fearing that one day he might end up in the defendant's seat. The hitman felt some sympathy for the defendant. The prosecution had made a good case against Alfred Saxon, but not an excellent one. Certainly enough for a conviction, but Argus was on the fence if it was enough for the death penalty.

The crime was heinous, the brutal murder of a woman who was a federal judge who had been presiding over his trial for racketeering. There was a blurry video from an ATM across the street, but the murderer's face was hidden by a hood. A traffic cam placed Saxon's car in the area at the time of the crime, but there were witnesses who swore the defendant was with them at the time of the crime, but the Assistant United States Attorney had proven with the aid of video surveillance that one of the witnesses was in a convenience store at the time he claimed to be with the defendant. Still, the other one might have been telling the truth, although Argus felt he was lying to help Saxon.

Argus had ways he would have questioned the man that would have gotten answers, but the court system frowned on jurors threatening a witness, even in order to get to the truth. It was enough evidence for a conviction and Argus had decided to vote guilty and for life imprisonment without parole.

Of course, the jurors had to discuss and review the evidence and testimony. Argus hadn't been thrilled about being sequestered. He didn't like anybody dictating's his comings or goings. There was no way around it without drawing undue attention to Jeff Costello.

The hotel wasn't a fancy one, but like all things with the government was probably the one with the lowest bid. While most of his fellow jurors looked on the civic duty as a chore, the elderly Mrs. Mackey looked on it as an adventure. She took her duty very seriously and had taken pages of notes on the yellow legal pads supplied all the jurors. She sat next to Argus in the juror box.

The food they got them wasn't bad. That night it was a hero sandwich of their choice, an apple, some chips and a couple of cans of soda. A US marshal knocked on the doors, gave them the food and reminded them that all jurors were expected to stay in their own room.

Mrs. Mackey wasn't having any of that. She and Argus shared a wall and a couple of minutes after the sandwiches were delivered, there was a knock on the connecting door.

Argus also didn't like having to go through a metal detector at the court every day. It limited his choice of weapons. Still, he had a small ceramic gun and ceramic knife. He pulled the knife out of its leg sheath and hid it behind his back as he opened the door. The small protective bar kept it from opening all the way until the expected face greeted him.

"It's only me, Jeffrey. There isn't a reason for a big strong man like you to be afraid of a little old lady now, is there?"

Despite himself, Argus smiled. "Depends on the little old lady."

"At my age, I never know how many more meals I have left and I do hate to dine alone. I know we're not supposed to, but would you mind if we ate together again?"

"Not at all, Mrs. Mackey." It had become a tradition for them, but Argus didn't let down his guard for anyone. "Let me shut the door so I can undo the latch."

Argus shut the door and replaced the knife in its sheath. When he reopened the door, he stepped into the senior citizen's room. She had taken one of her silk scarves and put it over a small nightstand that should've been by the bed, but had been slid to the middle of the room, along with a rolling chair that went with the desk.

"I do like to dine in style. Would you mind bringing the chair from your room in?"

"Already ahead of you, Mrs. Mackey." Argus rolled it in and sat across from the white-haired woman as she set down a pair of coffee mugs on the nightstand.

Argus set his sandwich down, then picked up Mrs. Mackey's can of soda.

"May I pour?"

The old woman smiled. "Why certainly."

Argus popped the top of the can. "Would you like to sniff the can? Should I let it breathe for a moment or just pour?"

"I think just pour." Argus did and the old woman giggled like a teenager. "I feel so naughty. It's not like me to break the rules, but for the third week, I'm spending part of my night in a hotel room with a handsome young man. The girls that I play canasta with will be so jealous when I can finally tell them."

Argus smiled and raised his mug. "You tell them what you like. I won't let them know any different."

The white-haired woman giggled. "So, Jeffrey, do you think he's guilty? Do you think he killed the judge?"

"Mrs. Mackey, we're not supposed to talk about it until we are in the deliberation room, which won't be until tomorrow morning."

"I know, but I think he did it. Now I tell you, I for one am not going to let him get away with it. I'm sending his tush to the pokey."

Argus smiled and lifted his mug of soda. "So am I."

Mrs. Mackey raised her mug and they clinked. Then there was

another clink as the door to Mrs. Mackey's room opened and two young men in suits walked in. One held a hotel master key which he put in his pocket as he shut the door behind them.

"Looks like the old lady's got herself a little bit of side action," said the one with the ponytail.

"Naughty, naughty old lady," said one with the scar across his forehead. Argus was already standing between the pair and Mrs. Mackey.

"Gentlemen, you obviously have the wrong room. I think you should leave now or we'll call the US Marshals."

"We own those two marshals. We got video evidence of the two of them screwing on duty while guarding somebody. We show that and their careers are ruined. They wandered off to use the bathroom and shut down all the cameras on this floor and the rest of the hotel for the next hour, so they ain't going to help you."

"If you know what's good for you, you'll leave anyway."

"Listen to Mr. Tough Guy tell us what to do. Who do you think you are?"

"I'm…" He had to force himself not to say Vince Argus. "…Jeff Costello."

"You say that like we should know you," Ponytail said. "You on a reality show or something."

"Or something. I'd call it 'You Bet Your Life' and the odds right now are stacked against either of you winning. There is no secret word, no duck coming down, no hundred dollars coming your way."

"You have any idea what he's talking about?" Ponytail said.

"None. But you know what, he's on the jury list too. We can kill two birds with one stone. We're here to tell you to make sure that you vote to find Mr. Saxon not guilty tomorrow," Scar said.

"Why on Earth would we do that?" Mrs. Mackey said.

"Because if you don't something bad may happen to you," Ponytail said. The pair opened their jackets, revealing guns in holsters.

"I'm not afraid of you," Mrs. Mackey said.

"Oh no?" Scar said, holding up a phone. On it was a picture of a smiling family playing in their backyard. "Then maybe something will happen to them."

"Are you threatening my son and my grandchildren?" Mrs. Mackey demanded.

"No threat, just a consequence. You don't do what we tell you to do and something bad is going to happen to them. Easy peasy. There only needs to be one dissenting vote for there to be a hung jury."

And the thugs figured the old lady would be the easy to intimidate.

"I'll tell the court. I'll tell the police," Mrs. Mackey said.

Scar shrugged. "It's our word against yours and we got two US Marshals who will say nobody came in here, plus a dozen guys who will swear that we were with them all night. And one of them will then pay your grandchildren a visit."

"Lay off the nice lady, boys," Argus said.

Scar and Ponytail turned their attention on the Soul for Hire.

"You're a tough one to crack, Jeff. You don't seem to have any family. Nobody we could threaten, which is why we didn't pick you. You seem to care about this old bag, so if you don't listen we're still going to hurt her grandkids. And what kind of a freak wears sunglasses indoors at night?"

"The last kind of freak you ever want to meet."

The pair made a big deal out of laughing. "Just remember, Mr. Saxon is not guilty or those little grandkids pay the price," Scar said, grinning wildly like an idiot. The two men exited the hotel room, shutting the door behind them.

"Mrs. Mackey, I'm going to follow them," Argus said.

"Jeffrey, it's too dangerous."

"I'll be okay."

Argus went back into his room and put on gloves. Next, he picked up his yawara stick, a Japanese weapon held in the palm of the hand. Nothing about it appeared extraordinary. It was plastic and some might even have difficulty believing it was a weapon, which is how he'd gotten it past the Marshals. Argus had his modified so it was also a pen, so he could explain it as a curiosity.

He also picked up his unopened can of soda. The hitman still had the ceramic gun and knife on him, but some situations called for something quieter that wouldn't leave evidence behind.

He went out the door of his room. Having not checked out the hotel himself, he worked on the assumption that the pair were telling the truth about the cameras in the hotel being down. The marshals were supposed to be on either end of the hall, but they were nowhere to be seen.

He saw the pair get on the elevator, so Argus took the stairs quickly. When he got to the fire door of the stairwell, he peeled off a piece of duct tape wrapped around a credit card sized piece of plastic he kept in his wallet and taped the locking mechanisms so he'd be able to get back inside.

There was a cab waiting outside the hotel in the rain with its meter running. In hopes of throwing off any description of him the cabbie might later give police, Argus took off his sunglasses and put his hair up in a bun. Argus limped over to the driver and spoke with a slight British accent. "You waiting for two guys, one with a ponytail and another with a scar on his forehead?"

"Yes."

"Turns out they're going to be a while, so they sent me to settle up for them. How much they owe you?"

The cabbie looked at the meter. "$72.13."

Argus pulled a hundred out his wallet and handed it to the cabbie. "Keep the change."

The cabbie took off and Argus ducked and limped in front of an alley. He noticed a camera as he went by. He picked up a bit of cracked sidewalk and went back to the alley and smashed the lens with a pitch so accurate the Yankees would have recruited him on the spot. The two men came out of the hotel, looked around and made a big show of cursing and waving their arms around at the lack of their cab. Argus put the sunglasses back on and stepped into the shadows.

The pair tried to flag another cab down, but it was raining so there wasn't another in sight. They turned and started walking in the direction of the alley where Argus was waiting.

When they passed the mouth of the alley, Argus took his sunglasses off and said, "Hey losers, we're going to vote your boss guilty. We may even ask for the death penalty now." Argus was trying to get the paired riled up and it worked. They turned into the alley and Argus backed up slowly.

"Then I guess Jeff that maybe you'll just disappear and they'll have to go with an alternate juror," Scar said.

Ponytail lunged first, but Argus hit him in the throat with the tip of the yawara stick, then swung his hand so the other end of the stick struck the thug at the back of his neck, smashing the atlas, the highest cervical vertebrae. It was rammed into the man's brain stem. Ponytail collapsed, no longer able to control his arms and legs. Not that it mattered much because his windpipe had been crushed. Suffocation would end his life in a moment.

Argus watched as Scar tried to get his gun out of his holster, but the Soul for Hire was more interested in watching the veins pulsing in the thug's neck. The hitman threw the can of soda at the left side of the man's chest. The blow was in sync with his pulse and hit so hard that it induced ventricular fibrillation, making the man's heart flutter instead of contract. The thug fell to the ground, holding his chest. An electric shock could have saved him, but instead, he got a different kind of shock as Argus stomped on his chest, breaking a rib clean through that then poked and tore his descending aorta.

As the two men lay dying, Argus wrestled the manhole cover in the alley and moved it out of the way. The hitman waited until he was sure both men were dead before he shoved their bodies through the opening and replaced the manhole cover. It wasn't the most efficient way to dispose of the bodies, but this hadn't been a planned job. He just had to hope they wouldn't be found until after the trial.

He went back into the hotel, removing his duct tape from the fire doors and climbing the stairs to his room. The marshals were still missing from their posts.

Argus hadn't bothered to close the connecting door, so as soon as he came back in, Mrs. Mackey rushed over.

"Jeffrey, are you okay?"

Argus nodded. "I couldn't find them."

"It's a good thing too. What are you going to do against two armed thugs?"

Argus tried not to smile. "You're right. I don't know what I was thinking."

"What are we going to do?"

"You vote your conscience. I'll vote not guilty," Argus said.

"Jeffrey, that would be wrong," Mrs. Mackey said.

"Not as wrong as your family being killed."

Mrs. Mackey took Argus' hand and held it to her cheek. "Thank you, Jeffrey. Such a good young man. I'm not feeling too well, so I'm going to go to bed now."

Argus nodded and closed the connecting door as the old woman went to sleep.

He took the pillows from the bed and positioned them under the blankets to look like a body, then he laid down on the floor on the far side of the bed. Argus was never a heavy sleeper. Anyone who tried to get in to come after him would go for the pillow body first, giving him enough time to take care of business.

Argus woke the next morning with no one having tried to break into his room. He showered and as he finished getting dressed there was a small, cautious knock on the connecting door. He opened it slowly. Mrs. Mackey was alone except for the tears in her eyes.

Argus frowned. "Are you going to be okay?"

Mrs. Mackey sniffled. "I don't know if 'okay' is the word I would use, but I am prepared to cast my vote to allow a guilty man to go free in order to protect my family."

"I'll be voting not guilty along with you."

"Thank you, Jeffrey." The woman grabbed Argus around the chest and squeezed him tight in a bear hug. The stony-faced hitman actually cracked a smile and hugged the old woman back. The marshals first knocked on Mrs. Mackey door, then Argus's.

Mrs. Mackey wiped her face and smiled as they shut the connecting doors and each one opened their respective doors to the hallway. The bus ride back to the courthouse was uneventful, although Argus looked at his fellow jurors, trying to figure out if any of the others had gotten a similar visit. He'd know soon enough by how everyone voted.

Twelve men and women reviewed the evidence. Both the prosecution and the defense had done a good job, but the video evidence of the crime was powerful. The forewoman of the jury called for a vote and everyone wrote it down on a piece of paper, folded it, then passed it down.

Turns out there were four votes of not guilty and by a quick exchange of guilty glances, Argus was able to figure out which two were visited by the two now dead thugs.

There was much spirited debate and then another vote was called.

An angry businessman with a belly and pricey suit rolled his eyes and groaned. Then he stared straight at Mrs. Mackey.

"Listen, Mackey, I know you're having a grand old time and probably voting no so you can get another night in the hotel, but some of us have lives to get back to. Jobs we have to do. So, stop messing around and vote the right way."

"You need to back off and apologize to Mrs. Mackey," Argus said in a whisper.

The businessman made a face, so used to dealing with underlings and interns that he had forgotten how the outside world works. "Or what?"

No longer in court, Argus had resumed wearing his sunglasses and he took them off and stared at the man. Argus had been told many times in his life that his eyes were terrifying. He didn't know if it was because of everything he'd seen, what he'd done, or because he'd sold his soul to the Devil that his eyes made people so nervous. He didn't much care. Argus just stared at the businessman until the man broke eye contact. Looking at the floor, he mumbled, "Sorry, Mrs. Mackey."

"The video shows the murder," the forewoman said.

"But not the man's face. And the one man says he was with the defendant. That's reasonable doubt, isn't it?" Mrs. Mackey said, almost pleading.

"It could be," Argus said. The two other jurors agreed. The debate raged back and forth the rest of the day and into the next. By the end of the second day, the forewoman sent word to the judge that they had a hung jury.

There were called into the courtroom.

"Madame Foreperson, have you exhausted all possibilities and avenues? Is there any way you all can come to an agreement?"

"No, Your Honor."

"Still I would like you to try for one more day."

The jurors did as instructed but the votes didn't change so at the end of the third day they returned to court.

"We are still deadlocked, Your Honor."

"I have no choice but to declare a mistrial. The defendant may remain free on bail. The prosecution is welcome to retry the case."

From the look on the defendant's face, you would've thought he had won instead of just getting a postponement. He looked at the jurors and smiled like he was running for office. His gaze lingered on the four jurors who voted not guilty. Mrs. Mackey and the other two turned away, but Argus meet his smiling stare with an icy one. Saxon turned away and slapped his lawyer on the back.

Alfred Saxon went to bed that night with a happy heart, but he woke up terrified, naked, and tied upside down to a table.

"Where am I? What's going on?"

Argus stepped forward and looked like a shadow in the darkness. "I changed my mind. You're guilty as sin. You killed that judge."

"That's for a court and jury to decide," Saxon said.

"Oh, I was on your jury," Argus stepped out of the shadows. "And now I'll be your judge and executioner too."

"You can't kill me. You don't have it in you, son."

"Just like you claimed to not be able to kill the judge. And I'm sure you had nothing to do with those two thugs who threatened to kill jurors' family members," Argus said.

"How do you know about that? You weren't on their list."

"Doesn't matter, but it made sure you're on my list."

"You can't get me for this. There's no proof. I never even talked to those two guys. My lawyer took care of it all. Don't blame me, blame George Fallow."

"Alfred, you son of a bitch, selling me out like that," came another voice. Argus flipped on the light, which revealed his naked lawyer in a similar inverted predicament across the room.

"You should have taken what the court was going to give you. I would've done my civic duty and gone home. But no, you had to threaten the family of a lady I liked. Now, I have to do what's right to make sure she and her family are safe. And I've already talked to your lawyer. Turns out you're not the first client he had these thugs talk to a jury for, which is why he's here. You don't have to worry about the two of them. They'll never be tampering with another jury again."

"Please don't do this," Saxon begged.

Argus took off his sunglasses, flipped the tables so they were back on the ground and took turns looking them both in the eyes.

"That's just what the judge mouthed on that video before you killed her. I'll gladly show you the same respect you gave her."

Argus walked over to the lawyer.

"I'm very wealthy. I can pay you to let me go."

"Turns out I'm wealthy too, so I don't need your money."

George Fallow acted just like he would have in court. When the first motion is shot down, make another. "A gentleman like you may need a lawyer someday. I will represent you for free."

"Thanks, but should that ever happen, I'll make sure I get a good lawyer."

Argus pulled on a rope which untied the lawyer. He stepped across the way and did the same for Saxon. They both got to their feet.

"You are letting us go? Saxon said.

"Nope. Just building a cover story about you two being lovers so your murder-suicide won't raise too much suspicion." Argus pulled a gun out, stood behind the lawyer and shot Saxon. He then grabbed the lawyer's right hand and put it on the gun and brought it up under his chin and fired again.

Turns out Fallow had a carry permit, so the hitman had used his gun.

He debated about using their phones to send a few fake but incriminating texts, but didn't want it to look staged. The cops would find them and draw their own conclusions.

Once he was sure they were dead, Argus left.

A few days later he met Mrs. Mackey for lunch. She gave him a hug and a kiss and they made small talk for some time.

"Did you see in the papers that Saxon and his lawyer were actually lovers that had a falling out, so Fallow shot Saxon then blew his own brains out?"

The police had drawn the conclusions Argus had hoped they would. They even found the other two thugs' bodies and launched an investigation, but so far nothing led back to Argus. Or Jeff.

Argus had also followed the pair of marshals that deserted their posts. They hadn't learned their lesson and Argus was able to record the pair having sex on the job. He sent the video to the marshal's anonymously, but promised to post it online if the matter wasn't handled by the US Marshals. The pair were jobless by the next day.

"I feel so relieved," Mrs. Mackey said.

"I'm glad to hear that," Argus said.

"My youngest son is gay. He married a wonderful young man. A doctor, no less. They adopted three kids and I'm very proud of them all. When he was a teenager, he was afraid to come out, but I saw how he acted around boys he liked and knew he was gay years before he told me. I was so happy when he finally trusted me enough to tell me the truth. I watched those two men in the courtroom throughout the trial. They didn't much care for each other, let alone find each other attractive," Mrs. Mackey said.

"Sometimes people can fool you," Argus said.

"Yes, they can," Mrs. Mackey said, putting her palm on top of Argus hand. "They found those two horrible men dead right underneath our hotel." Mrs. Mackey squeezed his hand. "Thank you, Jeffrey."

Argus tried and succeeded in looking confused. "For what?

Are you expecting me to buy lunch?"

"For protecting my family. It means more to me than you'll ever know."

Argus simply nodded.

"And if you're expecting an old lady to pay for lunch, you are no gentlemen. Maybe I'll leave the tip, though," Mrs. Mackey said.

Argus again smiled and had the most enjoyable lunch he'd had in years.

STOWAWAY

"Negral. Negral. Negral."

Vince Argus knew that was one way to summon Hell's Chief of Police. Although they'd met, the Soul for Hire had never called on the forgotten Sumerian god before and wasn't sure what to expect. The Chief had been a fire god, so Argus was half-expecting a ball of flame to suddenly appear.

The soft knock at the door took him by surprise.

Argus had taken great pains to make sure this small room was off the grid. It was thirty feet underground in an abandoned cement bunker off of a forgotten tunnel from the depression era, but still too close to the surface to attract attention from the Shadow Clan. It wasn't the type of place that had a lot of foot traffic or people knocking on the door to sell magazine subscriptions. It did have a video surveillance system and a generator. When he looked at the video monitor, all Argus saw was a cloud of smoke, which strangely then moved to form the words *You rang?* Then the smoke went away to reveal a man in a long trench coat, wearing a fedora and smoking a cigarette.

Argus slowly opened the thick metal security door and was face-to-face with one of the highest-ranking individuals in Hell.

"Argus."

"Chief."

The Soul for Hire stepped aside to let Hell's Detective walk into his workspace, but the chief stopped short when he saw the obviously beaten woman who was chained to a metal chair that in turn was bolted to the cement floor.

"Much as I might appreciate the gesture, these days I don't welcome human sacrifices," Negral said.

"That's okay. I'm not offering any."

The forgotten god frowned and stomped out his cigarette. "Why exactly did you call? Need help torturing your victim?"

"I've never enjoyed torture, but occasionally someone has some information I need. Usually, threats and intimidation are enough, but not in this case. I was hired to kill the individual who killed my client's husband."

The fire god's eyes narrowed as he stared at the woman in chains. "In this is the killer?"

"The killer plus one. I figure you know what that means."

The man in the fedora nodded. "The woman is possessed by a demon. It's obvious if you know how to look. But if her stowaway demon has only killed one person, unfortunately, that's within the terms of the Host-Horde Accord, although I personally frown on it."

Under the unwavering glare of Hell's Detective, the bound woman underwent a transformation from helpless victim to maniacal lunatic. Her eyes somehow got wider as she bared her teeth and began laughing hysterically.

"Hello, Chief. I assure you all my paperwork is in order. I've got a valid pass."

"I'm sure you do," Negral spat with disgust. "So, Vince, what do you want from me?"

"I want to know how to get the demon out and kill it."

"You're not an exorcist or a versatile mage, so it's probably beyond your abilities. Why do you want to know? Wouldn't killing the human host fulfill the terms of the contract you took?"

"Technically. However, I've vowed to not kill an innocent. The woman qualifies. I did a little research after I secured her here. It seemed her husband made a deal with her stowaway to get rid of his rival at work, who turned out to be the husband of the woman who hired me. The guy didn't even care that the demon took over his wife. Apparently, he even had sex with it before it went out to seduce and kill his rival. If I shoot her, she's dead and I have no idea what happens with the demon."

"Why come to me with this? I'm sure Nick would be happy to help you out."

"I've asked the Devil for information before. He's fine with giving it to me, as long as I agree to kill somebody for him in exchange. Problem is, the people he wants dead aren't people I want to kill."

"Innocents?"

"Some. Others aren't guilty enough to deserve a bullet. You've always been straight with me. You're not a demon. And your rep is good."

The fire god turned cop chuckled. "And what does my rep say about me these days?"

"Your word is as good as it gets. You deal fairly with those who aren't trying to screw you. And you're not in Hell because you want to be although the reasons seem to vary."

"What are the reasons they're saying?"

"You lost a bet. The Devil did you a favor. And my personal favorite – back in the 1940's you used up all of your power to save a group of your friends in the League of Shadows, so the Devil gave you enough manna so you didn't fade away to wherever forgotten gods go."

"Do you think information from me is going to be free?" Negral said.

Argus shook his head. "I don't, but I also don't think you will ask me to kill an innocent for you. I want to know how I can kill the demon but not the woman. What would you want in exchange for that information?"

"Now, Chief, I'm here on a legitimate visitor's pass. You don't want to be doing something to interfere with that now do you?" the woman said in a singsong voice.

"What I do or don't do doesn't concern you, so I'd advise you to shut your trap unless you'd like me to get involved personally and take a hands-on approach." The chief's hand burst into flame as he lazily wiggled his fingers around. Whatever was looking out from behind the woman's eyes seemed like it got a bit scared.

"Right you are, Chief. Shutting up now," the possessed woman said.

"Say I'm willing to provide you with information, are you willing to trade a favor to be named at a later date?"

"What would this favor involve?" Argus said.

"I'm not sure. I'd be willing to let you put stipulations in as to what you wouldn't be willing to do and see if I find that acceptable."

"Fine. I will not kill or otherwise harm someone I don't consider not deserving of it. I wouldn't want to do anything that has a high probability of getting me killed. I don't see any reason for Nick to collect my soul any sooner than necessary. I wouldn't want to do something that I found fundamentally wrong or something that would in some way, shape, or form harm my reputation."

"That's it?"

"Yes."

"Turn off your surveillance recording and let's step outside," Negral said.

Argus flipped a switch and followed Hell's Detective out the security door.

"Hurry back Argie-wargie. I'll miss you, snookums," the demon in women's clothing said.

Argus ignored it and slowly closed the door behind him.

"First thing you should know is you can't kill the demon. You can send it back to Hell or trap it, but that's as far as it will go," Negral said.

"I suspected as much, so I'll settle for information on how to do either of those two things," Argus said.

The man in the Fedora nodded. "You're no exorcist, so the only way you're going to get it out without killing her is to trick it. Unless you have the help of the person who made the deal in the first place. Can you get a hold of that person?"

"Not in working condition. I expect that when you get back downstairs, he'll be waiting in line to get in."

"That's unfortunate then. Your only option then is to trick it out. The problem is once it's out, it'll want to jump into somebody else. You're isolated down here, a good distance away from people up top and Mikoli's Shadow Clan below. That means the demon will want to jump into you, though I suspect you'd give it a good fight. Even so, I give you fifty-fifty odds about whether or not you win. Imagine the damage a demon could do with your abilities. Or even if it just kept jumping between bodies and killing along the way. It's never pretty."

"Then how do I trap it so it can't hurt anyone else?"

Negral met Argus's eyes and the hitman felt like the fire god could see right through his sunglasses and into his soul. Argus wasn't sure what he saw, but apparently, it had been enough. "Convince the demon that you're going to kill its host. It's tough, but if you managed to kill her before it jumps, it could spend a little time trapped in the corpse, up to about three days. It could still manage to walk the corpse around like it was a type of zombie."

Argus shivered. "This wouldn't be the type of zombie that can knit itself back together after you shoot it, would it?"

Negral tilted his head. "No, it wouldn't. However, if you convince it to jump ahead of time, it will try to possess you." Negral took a crystalline sphere about the size of a golf ball out of his pocket. "However, if you have one of these primed and ready, it'll suck it right in and trap it."

"What is it?" Argus said.

"It's a soul cage, very useful in trapping the essence of a person or demon."

"It would be trapped in there, unable to get out?"

The god in the fedora nodded. "It would take somebody with the power and the knowledge to open it up. I make them pretty durable, so it's unlikely it'll be smashed and broken. Of course, it's best to secure the area and encircle the demon within a spell circle. That way if it doesn't work, the demon can't get out and possess anyone else."

"How do I make one of these spell circles?"

"For you, it is possible. Your ability to hit any target is magical in nature, so you'd be able to activate a circle by hitting it, but you'd need specially prepared chalk. There's a woman over in Bed-Stuy who makes some for sale. There's another five people in Manhattan, two in the Bronx and one in Queens and maybe a few more that I've heard about but they're not as skilled. Somebody with enough power could just use regular chalk or even paint, but it's damn foolish for someone who's not trained. You draw a circle around what you want to contain, making sure there's no breaks in the line. You activate it either with a touch of your power or a drop of your blood. I recommend the power. Safer for you." Negral wrote down some addresses on a piece of paper and handed it to the hitman.

"I've got it chained up pretty good, but if I go to get some of this chalk, is there a chance it'll manage to get free while I'm gone?"

Negral nodded. "It's a very real possibility. To them, the body is no more valuable than a rental car a human has with insurance on. Damage to the body doesn't matter if it can get them where they're going."

"What about the soul cage? Where can I pick up one of those?"

"That's a bit harder. I don't know of anyone who has one for sale. You'd have to find someone with the power and the ability to make it."

"How about giving me that one? And a piece of that chalk if you have it."

"I make spell circles with fire, but I do keep a couple pieces of chalk in my pocket for emergencies. One piece tends to run about five grand. I'd break off a piece big enough for what you need for about five hundred. The soul cage takes me a very long time to make. I put the value of it at half-a-million."

Argus gave a long, slow whistle.

"That's a lot of scratch."

The Chief nodded. "There's a lot of craftsmanship and work that goes into making a soul cage. It's a fair price."

"It's more than I have easy access to. In my line of work, you have to hide money. Hard to explain to the IRS what I do for a living. I can get it, but it will take me a few days. What other options do I have? The guy he had killed has four kids. You know my history. No kid should lose a parent to a murdering bastard, human or otherwise. That makes it personal with me."

"Kids huh?" Negral blew out a thick cloud of smoke even though he had put out his cigarette inside the bunker minutes before. "It's refreshing to be called in by someone who's not a lowlife only looking out for themselves. I admire what you're trying to do here. I'll let you have this one for two hundred thousand."

"That's still several times more than I'm making for this job, but this bastard needs to pay. Thank you."

Negral handed him a business card with a bunch of numbers on the back. "That's my account. Sometimes having access to cash can be helpful."

Argus chuckled. "Never thought about it. I guess I always assumed that Hell gave you access to as much money as you needed."

"If it's Hell related business. Things of personal nature are another matter."

"I guess even Hell's chief of police has to have a personal life. I'll transfer the money in by the end of the day if that's okay."

The god in the fedora stroked his chin. "Your word on it?"

"Barring technical difficulties, yes, my word that I will transfer the money as soon as I can. So, do you need me to sign a deal in blood like Nick did?" Argus said.

Hell's Detective grinned and put his palm out. "Handshake will do. Your rep is pretty solid on keeping your word as well. And you're smart enough not to die for a couple hundred grand."

Negral handed over the soul cage and a piece of white chalk so pure Argus swore it glowed.

"Drawing a circle around her inside the bunker would give away the element of surprise." Argus looked around. "Does the line have to be all on the ground?"

Negral inspected the outside of the small bunker that was built into a wall of cement. "I guess it would be hard to draw a circle around and through a solid wall. As long as she's within the circle it can work, it's just not going to be anywhere near as strong. If you don't catch the demon before it possesses you, it will get out. It'll take it a few hours, maybe a day tops, instead of a couple months."

"If it doesn't work then it'll only be delaying the inevitable. A day or a month and it'll still be loose."

Argus drew a very uneven circle around the sides and front of the bunker, up the wall making it higher than the bunker roof, then down the other wall until the lines met.

"How does the soul cage work?"

Negral laughed. "That's probably way beyond your skill sets. I'll prime it for you so it's ready. For this to work, you're going to have to touch the demon spirit with the soul cage. Which is going to be difficult because they tend to be on the invisible side unless the demon is trying to be seen."

"Great. I can't hit something I can't see. Even with my powers."

"But you have an advantage that most humans don't. Because of your deal with Nick, you're attuned to things from the Pit, which is probably what gave you the suspicion that she was possessed in the first place. You should sense when it's jumping out and, if you focus, you'll be able to sense where it is. You have to hit it *before* it gets into you, a window of maybe a couple of seconds. You should also know that in that time it's going to be able to feel the soul cage pulling on it like a strong undertow. You don't have the kind of power needed to suck it in from a distance, so you must make contact quickly."

"Negral, I appreciate this."

Hell's Detective nodded. "Just don't mess it up. I'll even help you set the stage. Just don't trigger the circle until I'm on the outside."

"How exactly do I do that?"

"Think about how you use your power," Negral said, his eyes lingering on the hitman's guns.

Argus nodded in understanding.

Hell's Detective whispered the rest of his plan. Argus nodded and the pair went back into the bunker.

"What good was calling you? I don't know any bloody exorcists," Argus screamed.

The fire god shrugged. "Not my problem. You still got another option."

"But it's the same option I had before I did any of this," Argus shouted.

Negral lit another cigarette. "Too bad. But if you do it, the demon goes straight back to Hell." Negral turned so his back was to Argus and winked at the demon in woman's skin and clothing. She had to force herself to stop grinning wildly.

"I wanted to save the woman, not kill her."

"Not my problem. Good luck." Hell's Detective blew a puff of smoke and headed out the door.

Argus followed him out. "You're just as bad as your boss, you know that?"

"Got a nickel? Call someone who cares."

The door closed behind them. The god in the fedora triggered the soul cage and gave it to the hitman. Argus nodded once the forgotten god was on the other side of the chalk line. Negral nodded back.

Argus pulled his silencer-equipped gun and fired at the line, triggering the spell circle. He removed the silencer, then replaced the bullet in the chamber with one from a special pocket in his long black jacket before he went back inside the bunker, the gun in his right hand and the soul cage hidden in the palm of his left.

He took his sunglasses off and hooked them on the front of his shirt with his left index finger and thumb.

The woman looked at him frantically, tears streaming down her face. "What happened? Where am I? What's going on?"

"Veronica, is that you?" Argus wasn't buying it, but still, he had to make sure.

"That's my name. How do you know it? The last thing I remember is my husband asking me some weird questions and next thing I know I woke up here."

"I see. This must be very traumatic for you then," Argus said.

"You have no idea."

"I might." Argus put the gun back in its holster and pulled out a flask and put a drop onto the back of the woman's hand. It sizzled and smoked on contact

"Why would you pour acid on my wrist?" she screamed.

Argus put the flask back in his pocket and drew the gun again. "It's not. It's holy water."

"Damn. Too bad. I really thought I had a chance of making that work."

"You really didn't."

Argus was five feet away but he pointed the gun between the

eyes of the demon in women's clothing. "Veronica, I don't know if you can hear me in there, but I want you to know I'm sorry. I tried to save you but there's nothing else I can do."

"Wait a second. This is a healthy body. I've laid claim to it, fair and square. Can we negotiate? I don't know how much she's worth but I'm willing to sign all of it over to you. Plus, the bitch is pretty hot, right? And I know how to use everything she's got. Even her husband liked me better. Told me I did things to him that she never would."

Argus ignored the demon's ranting. "Goodbye, you no good bastard. Forgive me, Veronica."

Argus pulled the trigger and there was a loud bang.

Negral was right. Argus was able to feel when the demon left Veronica's body. He couldn't so much see it as sense a shimmering in the air as it leapt straight at him.

His left hand was already moving, throwing the soul cage right into what he hoped was the demon's essence. There was a sizzle and a sound that could have been screaming. Argus slowly and carefully picked up the orb and by squinting was able to make out the impression of a pair of angry eyes and horns within.

It worked.

Argus turned his attention to the woman in chains. "Veronica, are you okay?"

"I don't know about okay, but I'm better than I was with that thing inside me."

Argus nodded, pulled the bottle of holy water out of his pocket and poured some on her other hand. It just ran off her hand without sizzle or flame.

The hitman began the process of unbinding her.

"Thank you."

"You're welcome."

"But I don't understand. I saw you shoot at me," she said, as the hitman helped her to her feet.

"It was a blank. I usually keep a few on me. They come in handy more often than you might imagine."

"So, that scumbag that I married is really dead?"

"I don't know what you're talking about." That was what Argus said, but he nodded his head.

Veronica realized he didn't want to confess to murder but was grateful for the answer. "How can I ever repay you?"

"You wouldn't happen to have two hundred thousand dollars lying around, would you?"

CUTE AS
A BUTTON

"So you want me to take care of this?" Vince Argus asked, his eyes hidden behind shades as dark as night. His tone was as calm as it would be if he was ordering dinner.

"Not exactly," said Frank, the Rossa family consigliere.

"What then? I thought the business between Vinnie and me over what happened with Jimmy was settled," Argus said.

"Mr. Rossa has no quarrel with you and wanted me to relate that you were more than generous when you protected his daughter Abilyn for a week," Frank said.

"She's a good kid," Argus said, actually cracking a smile. Someone had been threatening Vinnie "The Rose" Rossa's family. Vinnie asked Argus to keep his five-year-old daughter safe. As Argus had lost his own family when someone made a move on his father, he would have taken the job even if it hadn't helped clear up the mess Argus had made with Vinnie's son Jimmy. Children and families should never pay for a man's crimes. A week with a five-year-old girl was something very different for the hitman, but he enjoyed it more than he would ever admit. The Soul for Hire had a soft spot for kids.

"Mr. Argus, Vinnie would like to ask you to do a job for him, just name your price," Frank said.

"What does he need?" Argus asked, far too gone from his long-lost innocence to agree without hearing the details.

"Someone has taken Abilyn," Frank said, watching as Argus' face changed from its normal stony look to one of barely controlled fury. The last time Frank had seen that expression was years ago when the hitman had been searching for his family's killers. Only after he delivered his vengeance did Argus evolve into the stone-cold taker of life he was today. "The kidnappers want five hundred thousand. We of course agreed. We dug up what we could; they are your basic wannabe thugs and have done this twice before. Once, the child was returned. The other time, the parents gave all they had, but it wasn't as much as the kidnappers demanded. The child was found shot two weeks later, in a dumpster. We are not going to do anything to risk Abilyn. The kidnappers insisted the ransom be delivered by a single man who was not a member of the family. Vinnie trusts you and would be deeply appreciative if you would handle this for him."

"Done. You want me to end this my way?" Argus asked.

"Personally, I would love nothing more, but part of the deal is that they walk out alive. The agreement must be followed. Vinnie and I gave our word that neither he nor I would order their deaths. And you know that includes any of our associates," Frank said. "This is contingent on them not hurting the girl. If they harm one hair on Abilyn's head..."

"The Devil himself won't be able to protect them from me," Argus said.

"Agreed," Frank said. His tone had more than a hint of approval in it.

"Where and when is the drop?"

The phone rang.

"Looks like we're about to find out," Frank said, pushing the speaker button on the phone. "Good afternoon."

"Hey Fink boy, I mean Frank. You have what we want?" a voice said, trying to be manly and tough on the other end. The end result was close, but not quite there.

"We do. Now let me speak to Abilyn," Frank said.

"She can't come to the phone right now," the man said.

"Why?" Frank asked, fighting to keep his tone even through gritted teeth.

"Chill, she's fine. She just kept singing this stupid song over and over and wouldn't shut up. We had to gag her to get her to be quiet."

"Ungag her now and bring her to the phone," Frank ordered.

"Relax. We'll get her."

"Hello," came the voice of a little girl whose tone indicated that she was handling things quite well.

"Abilyn, this is Uncle Frank. Are you okay?"

"I guess, but these men are mean. They took me right out of the locker room at tap class and wouldn't even let me put my shoes on. I still have my tights on."

"Have they hurt you?" asked Frank.

"No, but they wouldn't let me bring my knapsack or my shoes or anything."

"What song were you singing?" Frank asked, trying to learn if the kidnappers were telling the truth.

"I wasn't cursing or anything," the girl said, worried she was about to get in trouble.

"I believe you. I'd just like to know what it was," Frank said. Abilyn sang in Italian something that roughly translated as "Poophead, poophead, you're a stinky poophead." Argus and Frank smiled at each other. The girl wasn't intimidated by the thugs; she was tormenting them.

"I'm going to send Mr. Argus to come get you, but I want you to be a good girl and stop teasing those men," Frank said.

"I like Mr. Argus. He's a lot of fun. He even let me braid his hair," Abilyn said pretending not to hear Frank's request. Frank gave Argus a glance, but the revelation didn't break the Soul for Hire's legendary cool. "Would you please have him bring my shoes?"

"He'll have them. Put the man back on the phone, sweetheart," Frank said.

The man's voice returned. "Told you she's fine. We got a deal? Five hundred large, you get the girl, we walk away, and you don't send anybody after us. Ever."

"We have a deal, provided Abilyn is unharmed. The slightest injury and our arrangement will be over. That includes gagging her," Frank said.

"She'll be fine." The kidnapper gave the address of an old abandoned garage, and a time an hour and a half in the future, then hung up.

Frank pushed a briefcase across the table. "It's all in here. What fee—"

Argus lifted his hand. "Don't insult me by offering me money."

Frank nodded his head. "Thank you."

Argus nodded back and handed Frank a bullet cartridge with his name engraved on it. Frank had done this enough times before to not even blink an eye. "I swear on this bullet and my life that everything I have told you is true."

Frank handed Argus back the bullet that would kill him if he was lying. The hitman slipped it into his pocket.

"I'll have Vito and a couple of the guys drive you. You will go in alone; they will wait in the car for Abilyn."

They got to the drop site early. Argus got out a block away to scout the area and make sure no traps were waiting for him.

There was nobody outside the building. Argus returned to the car to wait.

At the appointed time, he got out carrying the briefcase. The door was caked with grease and grime. He could see someone looking out through a rubbed away peephole. The door creaked open.

"C'mon in, tough guy," said a man in his early twenties, his arms covered with tattoos, his hands caked with oil and dirt. He closed the door behind him. "You got our money?"

"First, the girl walks out," Argus said, opening the case so they could see the cash.

The man nervously motioned to his partner, who stood next to a backroom door. The partner had a dozen piercings on his face and a bandanna tied around his head. He motioned and Abilyn walked out.

Her face beamed when she saw the hitman. "Mr. Argus!"

The girl ran toward him and wrapped her arms around Argus. The Soul for Hire returned the little girl's hug. "Are you a-okay?" he said, knowing from their week together that it was one of her favorite terms.

"Yes. Did you bring my shoes?" she asked.

"Of course." Argus handed the footwear over.

The little girl put them on after taking off her tap shoes. "That's better."

"Your Uncle Vito is waiting for you outside to drive you home. Go now," Argus said.

"Okay," she said, motioning him to bend so she could whisper in his ear. "They didn't hurt me, but they were mean and not very smart." Argus opened the door, and she went out after saying, "Bye-bye, meanies." And then she sang her little song.

The two men walked up to Argus and each nervously handed him a button that looked like it had been ripped from Abilyn's sweater. "The girl said we had to give you these to get the money."

Argus was floored by the stupidity of the pair and the deviousness of the girl. He passed them the money. The kidnappers flipped through the bills quickly, getting very excited at their ill-gotten windfall. "You still here, tough guy?"

"We still have business, the two of you and me," Argus said.

"No, we don't," the one with piercings said.

"Do you know what giving me that button meant?"

"No," the one with the tattoos said.

"Sometimes it is unwise to come out and say things when you want something illegal done. Symbols are used instead," Argus said.

The men realized something was going wrong and pulled their guns, but Argus drew and shot each of them in the hand first, making them drop the weapons. The Devil may have gotten the better end of the deal in their bargain, but what the Devil gave Argus made sure he never missed. Some people would consider that worth a soul. Vince Argus had never commented either way on the matter.

"When Abilyn told you to give me the buttons, she was putting a hit out on you, and she got you to deliver it to me in person. What dumb bastards. You may be the stupidest people on Earth," Argus said.

"We had the consigliere's word he wouldn't have us killed!" screamed tattoo boy, clutching his bleeding hand to his chest.

"True, which meant you were going to get to walk unless

someone higher up said otherwise," Argus said.

"The Rose never said nothing," tattoo boy said.

"No, he didn't, but the agreement was that The Rose and his people wouldn't hurt you. If you had bothered to learn anything about your victim, you'd know that despite her age The Rose's daughter holds a higher rank than The Rose's consigliere. And she's not involved with any of his business dealings. Her orders aren't covered by the deal," Argus said, a gun in each hand pointed at each kidnapper's head.

"C'mon, have mercy," begged tattoo boy.

"Like you did on the second child you kidnapped?" Argus asked.

"We didn't want to kill him, but they didn't come up with all the ransom. It was just business," groveled tattoo boy.

"Pity. That little girl is a friend of mine, which makes this personal. Give the Devil my worst," Argus said.

Outside, the little girl in the car couldn't hear the twin pops of silencers as two bullets ended both kidnappers' lives, but she smiled and waved as she watched the Soul for Hire walk out of the garage. Argus smiled and waved back.

ACT OF
CONTRITION

The church was almost empty. Most of Father Fayes's Tuesday afternoon regulars had already been in to see him, but there was still a good hour left in his schedule so the priest waited in the center chamber of the dark confessional. Fayes enjoyed this part of his duties. He thought that he was a good listener and apparently so did many others. In the booth to his right, he heard the familiar rustle of the curtain and a loud *thunk* as someone knelt down. Father Fayes gently drew aside the window, opening the confessional screen. There was an outline of a young man in the shadows. Whoever it was remained silent.

Doing his best to help overcome the confessor's nervousness, the priest opened the conversation. "How long has it been since your last confession?"

"It's not my sins I'm here to talk about, Father," said the man. In the dark, the priest's eyebrows shot up over his forehead.

"Argus!" the priest whispered, despite the fact that the confessional was designed to muffle sound in order to keep conversations private. "Did you do it?"

"You mean did I kill the young man who you said was stalking you and threatening your life?"

"Yes."

There was an extended moment of silence in the confessional during which the priest squirmed uncomfortably. Even though they were barely visible, there was something unsettling about the eyes of the man staring at him.

"Before we discuss the fate of the young man in question, why don't we discuss the story that you told me." Reaching out with his right hand, Argus slid aside the screen. The newer confessionals were designed to be able to accommodate both private and face to face conversations. With his left hand, he placed a cartridge on the ledge between them. On it was engraved *Fr. Benjamin Fayes.* "You remember this bullet, don't you, Father?" The priest swallowed hard and nodded. "You swore to me on this bullet that your story was true."

On the priest's forehead, beads of perspiration started to coalescence. Fayes formed a smile. "Of course, I remember. Everything I told you is true. I'm a priest. I wouldn't lie. You know that, don't you?"

Argus continued as if the priest had never spoken. "I did a little checking of my own. The man you claimed was threatening you was doing just that, but not exactly in the way you said. There was no threat to your life, no danger of him gunning down your parishioners. He was only trying to blackmail you."

"Only? Sure, it started out as blackmail, but I couldn't – no, I wouldn't pay. That's when the death threats started."

The priest was cut short by the first burst of emotion he had ever seen in the man. Unfortunately, the emotion was anger.

"No lies. Not here."

"I wouldn't think a man in your profession would be terribly concerned about what happened in a church."

"And I would think that a man of the cloth *would* be concerned about what happened in the house of God. And in God's name. This kid never threatened your life. He never asked you for money. He simply wanted you to leave the priesthood."

"The priesthood is my life. I wasn't going to walk away from everything I am just because some punk told me to."

"That punk says you sexually molested him for years when he was a kid."

"He's lying. He's jumping on the bandwagon with all the news about the tragedies in the Church. He was just looking for some attention and some cash. I never touched the liar."

"That's not how he tells it."

"It's his word against mine."

"Not exactly," Argus said, letting his last sentence hang in the air. In that moment, there was no sound in the confessional and

Fayes learned a new meaning of eternity. The priest fancied himself tough and decided to try to wait it out, but he couldn't do it.

"What do you mean 'not exactly'?"

"It seems you couldn't stop at just this one kid, if you want to call a twenty-year-old a kid. To hear him tell it, you hadn't touched him in years."

"I tell you I haven't touched him ever."

Argus put his outstretched index finger across his lips and the priest obeyed the silent order.

"Sadly, he had a twelve-year-old brother and it turns out you couldn't keep your hands off him either."

"How dare you! I knew and loved that boy."

"A little too biblically if you ask me."

"He has no right to sully the memory of his brother like that."

"This would be the same brother who just two weeks ago committed suicide using his father's gun to blow his brains out? The same boy whose funeral you presided over?"

"Yes, his death came as a terrible shock to all of us. It's a tragedy when someone so young does something so horrible."

"You sound so damn sincere." Argus shook his head disdainfully. "Doesn't the Church consider suicide a mortal sin, one that will bar him from heaven?"

"I like to think of God as being able to forgive all sins."

"Me too, but we both know better. Hell is a popular destination."

"What do you know about Hell?" said the priest scornfully.

"I know it's real and I know for sure that the Devil exists. There's a deal I made long ago that one day I'll have to answer for, so I'll end up giving the Devil his due. But I'm not the only one here in that boat."

"I've had no dealings with the Devil."

"Maybe not directly. The twenty-year-old kid you wanted me to take out for you told me what you had done to his brother and that was the reason he committed suicide."

"I feel terrible for him, but in his grief, he's become delusional. He's searching to find a reason for what happened and has decided on me as his scapegoat. That's why he wants to kill me."

"The kid doesn't want to kill you. He just never wants you in a position to hurt another child ever again. I'm with him on that."

"Argus, don't tell me you're taking his word over mine? He's been in counseling for the better part of a decade."

"I wonder why? But it's not just his word against yours." Plastic scrapped along wood as a memory stick slid across the divide.

"What's that?" the priest asked.

"It's something that the kid you wanted dead found this morning. His brother didn't write a suicide note, he recorded it. There's every ugly detail about every sick, twisted thing you did to him. So, you see, it's the words of two people against yours. I'm betting that there are others who will come forward if someone else lights the way. But that's not all. The little brother snuck his new smartphone in his book bag the last time you molested him, you sick bastard. It has your voice talking to him, telling him what you wanted, how he shouldn't tell anybody. He played it for the camera."

The priest reached out, grabbed the memory stick and hugged it close to his chest. "Oh my God."

"Oh, He knows and I'm sure He's not too happy with you. You caused the death of a child. You took away the innocence of at least two children. Only He and you know how many more."

"You can't have this. I won't give it back to you."

"Keep it. It's a copy. Other copies will be headed out in about an hour to all the major news outlets."

"You can't do that."

"Watch me. Then there's a little matter of this," Argus said, picking up the bullet between his thumb and forefinger. "You swore to me on this bullet your story was true, knowing how I work, knowing that a lie would ensure that I would use this bullet to kill you. Well, you lied so it's time to finish the deal." Argus wiped his fingerprints clean from the casing and returned the bullet to the sill.

"You can't kill me. I'm a priest."

"I can and I will. You're a priest in name only. A real priest would die before doing what you've done. By the end of tonight, you will be dead and your reputation will be in ashes."

"Please, don't do this."

"You will die here and now. That much can't be changed."

"But you just said that this was the house of God and it should be respected. You can't kill me here."

"Somehow I think God will appreciate it. Although truth be told, I prefer not to have the blood of a priest, however evil, on my hands." Argus paused and Fayes leaned forward, hoping for a reprieve. "Perhaps I could give you another option for your demise."

Father Fayes was slumped, his pale skin balmy. "What?"

Argus reached into the pocket of his long black trench coat and took out a gun wrapped in a handkerchief. It was untraceable, but it fired the same caliber ammunition as the bullet it was placed next to. Argus' intention was clear.

"No. I won't kill myself. I'll go straight to Hell."

"I think you're going there anyway. Look at it like this, you'll get to use the express lane."

"Why would I ever even consider doing that?"

"Because if you do, I'll make sure that the video doesn't get shown to anybody."

The priest sat dumbly, sweat soaking through his stiff Roman collar.

"You promise that no one will see what's recorded on that drive?" demanded the priest.

Argus picked up the flash drive and slid it into his inside jacket pocket. "I'll make the drive and anything on it disappear."

"All right, I'll do it." The priest picked up the gun and stared numbly at it. Something so tiny felt very heavy in his hand.

"Do you have anything you want to say before?"

"Just make sure that no one ever sees that."

"I was hoping you might have an apology you wanted me to give somebody."

"I didn't do it, Argus."

"Yeah, right. That's why we're going through all this and you didn't keep up the denials once you saw the memory stick. Last chance. They say confession is good for the soul."

"Go to Hell."

"One day. Make sure you save me a seat," Argus said sadly. "I'll be waiting outside to make sure the deed is done."

Argus left the confessional without saying good-bye. Walking back, he stood in the rear of the church. Almost three minutes passed before he heard the loud bang from the confessional and saw the door splinter outward. Argus went down the center aisle, walked up to the crucifix in the front of the church and nodded.

"It's nice to finally do one for the other side."

Argus then genuflected, made the sign of the cross and exited through the side door of the church. Outside there was a garbage can attached to a street light. Argus reached in his coat pocket, pulled out the memory stick and dropped it in the can. A young boy walking by watched the process.

"Why are you throwing it out? What's on it?" the boy asked.

"Nothing. It's empty."

CONUNDRUM

"How dare you!" Jerry Greene said at the sight of the twin bullets. One was engraved with his name, the other his wife's.

The man in the black trench coat and dark sunglasses didn't react, save for lifting one eyebrow.

"This is insane. You can't come into my home and tell me that you're going to kill me and my wife if we lie to you. It's absurd," Jerry said. "You can't get away with this."

"Mr. Greene, you invited me here to talk about hiring me to kill somebody. What are you going to do, call the police? And I did not say I was going to kill you and your lovely wife. What I said is that in order to hire me, you and your wife both have to swear on those bullets that everything you tell me is true. Because if you lie, these bullets will be coming back to you at a very high rate of speed. That's no threat. It's a promise," Vince Argus said.

Jerry Greene looked sheepishly at his wife who had put her hands over her eyes and was quietly crying.

"You don't understand. After what happened, we've been a wreck. My wife took a bottle of sleeping pills. If I hadn't gotten home from work early and got her to the hospital in time to pump her stomach, she wouldn't even be here right now."

The Soul for Hire turned to look at Shirley Greene. The weight of his stare caused her to take her hands away from her face and look back.

"Loss can be horribly painful, but you have to make a decision. You decide to either live with the pain and work your way through it or you give up and leave this world. No one else can make that decision for you, but if you want to hire me, you need to make it now. I don't need the attention a suicide would draw anywhere near me. So, what's it going to be, Mrs. Greene? Are you going to go on living or are you crawling into your grave?"

"I can barely go on without my baby. I'm not sleeping, not eating."

"Then you need to seek help. That's not an answer."

"If you agree to kill the bitch that murdered my baby, you damn well better believe I'm going to live so I can spit on and then dance on her grave," Shirley said with an evil glint in her eye.

Vince Argus nodded. He knew very well that vengeance could motivate someone to go on living. He just found that most people weren't as well suited to taking it for themselves as he was.

A fly buzzed around Jerry's head and he swatted at it ineffectually.

"Why does it matter for us to swear on these bullets so much?" Shirley said.

"People hire me to kill other people. I'm very particular about the lives I take. There are many people who will lie about why they want someone dead. I only kill those that I feel deserve it. So, if someone has lied to me about the reason they want someone in the grave, that means I might kill someone who doesn't deserve to die. Swearing on a bullet keeps things simple. Now tell me the whole story."

"Madeleine Hankins killed my little Jimmy."

Shirley choked on her sobs, so her husband continued.

"The woman broke into our home and stole Jimmy right from his crib."

"How did she know where the baby was? Babysitter? Friend?" the Soul for Hire asked.

"Hardly. We had interviewed her as a nanny when my wife was pregnant. We gave her a tour of the house," Jerry said.

"How do you know it was her who kidnapped your baby?"

"I'm a light sleeper and I heard something on the baby monitor. And I went to investigate. I saw her trying to walk out with Jimmy and I screamed. Jerry came running with a death grip on one of his golf clubs and was about to smash her in the head. Hankins put her hands around Jimmy's throat and said if we came near, she'd snap his neck. She told us if we let her go, she'd leave Jimmy in the driveway. Jerry wanted to take her out, but I wouldn't let him. I wish I'd let him." Shirley Greene collapsed on her husband's shoulder, sobbing.

"We let her go and she ran down the driveway, but it had been raining and she slipped and fell right on top of Jimmy. The impact snapped his neck. Police say he died instantly."

"This sounds like it would be more appropriate for the police than me. Seems a fairly open and shut case," Argus said.

"You'd think that, but it wasn't. Turns out she had an alibi. She was sleeping with some judge who claimed she was with him all night. The man was seventy-two. Probably didn't even know what day it was, let alone what time. The police took the judge's word over ours because they couldn't find any forensic evidence. She was wearing gloves and must have gotten rid of the clothes she was wearing. For a time, they tried to blame it on us," Shirley said. "You know what it's like to have all my friends and family think that I killed my own baby? Local papers even ran with it, blaming it on postpartum depression."

"Why not simply have another child?" Argus asked.

"We would if we could. I'd have a whole houseful, but I was lucky to have Jimmy. I underwent fertility treatments for years before I was able to conceive and then we had four miscarriages. When I carried Jimmy to term, it was a miracle. During my pregnancy, the doctors found tumors when I got an ultrasound. I refused any chemo or radiation. The doctors all thought it safest if I delivered by C-section so they could also remove the tumors. It was extensive and they had to give me a hysterectomy. I can't have any more children," Shirley said.

"You could adopt," Argus said.

"We'd love to, but we can't afford it. We spent all our savings on the fertility treatments. Even took out a second mortgage," Jerry said. "We never considered ourselves the type of people who would have somebody else murdered, but this woman killed our son and destroyed our chance at a family. She ruined our lives and she gets away without any consequence? That's not right. The police aren't going to do anything about it. I considered trying to kill her, but I'm not even sure how I'd go about it. At least not without getting caught. If I was alone with this woman for just five minutes, I'm sure I could kill her, but then I'd go to jail. My life would be over."

"If you're broke, then how are you going to pay me?" the Soul for Hire said.

"We managed to put together $11,000. That wouldn't be enough to pay the lawyers for an adoption, but maybe it'll be enough for us to get some peace," Jerry said, holding up an envelope filled with hundred dollar bills. Argus took it and put it in his pocket. "Aren't you going to count it?

Argus' mouth curled into a half smile. "Neither of you strike me as being stupid or foolhardy enough to try and cheat me."

"When and how are you going to do it?" Shirley said.

"It's best that you don't know the details. I would recommend, however, working hard to account for all your time. Visit friends and family a lot. Go out to eat, make sure to pay by credit card. If you pass by a store that has a video camera, make sure you walk in front of it because the police will be looking at both of you as suspects. However, I'll do my best to make it not even look like a murder."

When Argus left, the grieving parents were sobbing and holding each other.

Argus did his due diligence about his target. Police reports backed up what the Greenes had told him. Maybelline Hankins didn't have a job, yet she didn't seem short on money. When she went out, he went in and examined her apartment and found seven separate IDs, each with Hankins' picture on it. A further check of her computer revealed multiple accounts for each of the identities, all of them having correspondence with couples who were going to adopt her baby. It didn't seem very likely that the woman was going to have septuplets.

Argus also checked the apartment for weapons. Besides a set of steak knives, Hankins kept a .38 revolver tucked between her mattress and box spring. Argus removed the bullets and put it back where he found it. Then he sat down to wait.

Less than an hour later, Hankins returned home.

Argus waited until she had shut and locked the door behind

her before he stepped out from around the corner.

Argus had his sunglasses off. Normal people felt uneasy when looking into his eyes, so he found it easier to keep them covered most of the time. He made an exception for those whom he killed. The hitman felt if he was going to take their lives, the least he could do is look them in their eyes.

He lifted up his gun with a silencer and pointed it between Hankins pupils.

"Why?"

"Your past has caught up to you," Argus said. One was never sure who might be listening and telling her why might expose his clients to the law.

Hankins turned on a combination of the waterworks and sex appeal, dropping to her knees and putting her hands together begging. "Please don't kill me, if only to spare my baby."

Argus gave her half a chuckle.

"Nice try, but you've got six couples on the line for a baby under fake IDs. You pretend to be pregnant and promise people a child, then you wait for someone else to have a baby and you kidnap the infant, passing the child off as your own. You've done this too many times for them all to be your children."

"But this time I really am pregnant. I have a pregnancy test in the bathroom. I'll take one to prove it.

"A grifter like you probably has special tests made up to prove you're pregnant when you're not. Probably helps reel your marks in."

"You're the first one to catch on to that," Hankins said with a smile. "I'd be happy to run up to the drugstore get another one."

Argus just stared at her. She tried to match his gaze but turned away after a few seconds. Part of the code he lived by meant never harming an innocent, especially a child. He had to make sure.

As part of the payment for his soul, Argus was able to hit any target, but wasn't able to break the laws of physics. He couldn't make a bullet curve around corners or go double the distance. Argus had studied human anatomy extensively. Movies and TV shows like to make people think that it was the easiest thing in the world to hit somebody in the back of the head and knock them out. It could be done, of course, but all too often the person knocked out could be killed, have brain damage, or simply have headaches or pain for the rest of their life. Plus, it left evidence on an autopsy.

Up close, there was an easier method. The carotid arteries had two different types of sensors designed to protect the brain. One reacted to a chemical change, the other to changes in blood pressure. In the latter, suddenly elevated blood pressure kicked in the receptor and made the brain lower blood pressure to help prevent a stroke or heart attack. A side effect was passing out. The sensors were hard to isolate, which is why soldiers and the like went for choke holds to make sure they had them. A few seconds of direct pressure knocks a person out. The hitman's methods were more precise than a choke hold. Argus reached up with his thumb and index finger to press on the points in Hankins' neck. She passed out and he caught her before she hit the ground. Using duct tape, he secured her to her bed, putting a sock in her mouth to keep her from screaming.

One of the key goals of the hitman was to blend in and not draw attention. Not to mention not leaving evidence of being in the area. Most drugstores and supermarkets had surveillance cameras which would show him getting a pregnancy test.

Argus needed to have somebody else get the test and make sure they remembered him quite differently. He left his guns and shoulder holsters, along with his long black trench coat in the apartment. He borrowed a large pink blouse and put it on over his clothes, then pulled his hair up into a ponytail. Next, he put on some clip-on earrings and a pair of rose colored women's sunglasses. Lastly, he put on a Hollywood grade fake mustache.

Hankins' apartment had no security, so he took her keys and went down the back stairwell and walked several blocks away until he found an area that had several chain drug stores within a few blocks. Argus began to walk with an affectation that was virtually a strut and changed his entire body language. With an effeminate air, he walked over to a pair of tween boys who were standing on a stoop with nothing better to do.

"You boys have to help me," he said a voice slightly higher than his normal base. "My girlfriend think she's pregnant."

The boys looked at each other, and then at Argus in disguise. "You like girls?"

Argus sighed with great exasperation and threw his head back, rolling his eyes. "Look, I'm going through an experimental stage, okay? I was hoping you boys would go buy a pregnancy test for me to bring back to her."

"Why can't you do it yourself?" asked one of the boys.

Argus leaned in to motion the boys closer and then said in a whisper, "Because I also have a boyfriend and he doesn't know about my girlfriend. You never know who you'll bump into. I don't want one of my friends to see me buying a pregnancy test and tell my snookums about my honeypie. Look, I'll give you twenty for the pregnancy test and another twenty when you bring it back to me."

The boys exchanged another look and smiled. "A hundred bucks."

"Thirty bucks. And you can keep the change from the twenty."

One boy started to open his mouth to barter. "Look, we both know you ain't the only kids on this block. We got a deal?"

"For thirty bucks, sure," the boy said.

Argus handed him a twenty. "Anyone asks, say you're buying it for your sister."

"I don't have a sister."

"Then it works out good for everybody, doesn't it? I'll meet you back here in ten minutes."

When the time passed, Argus returned still in disguise. When the boys handed him a white plastic bag, Argus opened it up and looked inside. It was a pregnancy test box. He put his hand inside the bag and opened the box to make sure there was one inside. There was.

Argus handed the boys a twenty and a ten, then gasped and pulled the bag close to his chest. "Thank you so much, boys. This means a lot to me."

The boy waved the bills in the air. "Us too. Hope she ain't

pregnant."

"You and me both," he said.

Argus got back and Hankins was still unconscious. He took the duct tape from her wrists and ankles, removed the gag, and slapped her awake, then marched her into the bathroom and handed her a pregnancy test.

"Little privacy, please?" Hankins said.

"Not happening."

"I can't go if anyone watches me," Hankins said, probably thinking that her slight eye flick to the window went unnoticed.

"Then turn on the faucet or think of a bubbling stream or babbling brook."

Hankins scowled, then dropped her pants, sat on the toilet and took the test. Argus had her put the test on the bathroom sink then lay down face first in the tub. It didn't make any sense to give her a chance at rushing him when he went to look at the results.

A short time later, the test showed a result. The conwoman was telling the truth. She was pregnant.

"See?" she said. "So, who sent you to kill me?"

Argus stayed quiet.

"Some parents found out I kidnapped the kid they adopted and freaked out because they might have to give back their precious baby?" Hankins said. "So, they want me dead so nobody will find out?"

Argus remained mum.

"So what now? You just kill me and my unborn baby?"

"To be determined," Argus lied. "How are you pulling this scam off? Mothers aren't allowed to make any money off an adoption officially, which means you have to have some sort of go-between to set things up for you."

Hankins turned her head from the bottom of her tub to look at the hitman. "I'm not about to tell you anything. Are you the type of man who can kill a pregnant lady?"

"No."

Argus held up the fake IDs and social security cards he'd found hidden around her apartment. He'd already copied all the emails onto a flash drive.

"But don't think you're going to be able to use any of these again," he said, throwing them in a bag that also held the pink blouse he'd worn.

Argus leaned into her tub and again pressed her throat, sending Hankins off into the land of the unconscious.

When the conwoman awoke, there was no trace of the Soul for Hire. Hankins searched her apartment, checking everywhere she had hidden a fake ID. The hitman had been good, but not perfect. Argus had left one ID behind. Hankins assumed he had missed it. It was a great hiding spot, between the paper cover and the plastic on the outside sleeve of a DVD case.

Which is exactly what Argus wanted her to think. If she was limited to one identity, it would be that much easier to track her down. Hankins transferred money to her only remaining alias's account, packed a bag and left town for points south.

Argus returned to tell the Greenes what happened. As he expected, they were none too happy that the woman who killed their son was still alive.

However, after Argus told the grieving parents his plan, they were willing to overlook this fact and ended up quite pleased.

Hankins, now Sally Jones, spent the next six months looking over her shoulder but saw no sign of the hitman. At one point, she tried to contact the lawyer who acted as a broker for her adoption scams in exchange for a third of the take. He had died in a robbery. Somebody took his wallet, watch, and a lot of his client files. She thought about trying it on her own and even contacted the nurse practitioner who had helped her to fake the ultrasounds in the past, but she had died in a freak accident. The woman had a thing about signing all her prescriptions with an old-fashioned fountain pen. It was her trademark. She tripped and fell and the pointy end of the pen ended up embedded in her throat when she hit the floor.

The new Sally Jones decided she would simply have the baby and then go looking for a couple to pawn it off on for a fee. There were plenty of rich couples looking for kids that could manage to pay her fifty to eighty grand in cash under the table to get a baby.

When the day came for the blessed event, Sally Jones insisted on a C-section. She wasn't about to go through hours of labor over some baby. Bad enough she was going to have a scar, but her OB/GYN promised her that her bikini bottom would cover it. The woman masquerading as Sally Jones acted like a happy mother, claiming that her husband was a soldier serving overseas and she was far away from her family, so none of them could make the birth. Her story got her a bunch of free baby clothes and toys from the nursing staff. It wasn't anything she could use, but she took it anyway. It was the principle of the con.

The conwoman had already spoken to a wealthy couple about the baby, claiming that she wasn't sure if she was ready for motherhood. Then she told them that the baby had been the result of a date rape and she didn't think she'd be able to be a good parent because every time she saw the baby she would think of what she'd endured.

When she told them she needed money to move away and start a new life, they offered her cash - sixty thousand. The conwoman pretended to have second thoughts and said that another couple had offered her more so they upped their offer to a hundred grand.

It was the jackpot and she wouldn't have to split it with anybody. Hankins figured she'd live a few more days as Sally Jones with the kid then make the exchange with the rich parents-to-be.

Hankins would move to somewhere nobody knew her and start a new scam. Or maybe go back to an old one where she hooked up with rich, married men, then pretended to be pregnant. That was when she had first started using the fake pregnancy tests. They'd give her money to go away, take care of the problem, anything she wanted as long as she didn't tell their wives. She had almost instantly gone down to her pre-pregnancy body and now her breasts were huge, which would help her rope in the men all the easier.

The rent for her Sally Jones apartment was paid through the end of the month. There was no reason to waste money, so she'd stay until then. She'd flirted with the landlord and he'd given her a deal. Maybe now that she was hot again, she could talk him into another free month with hints that he might get lucky. Some men were horny or desperate enough for that to work. She'd miss it when she left. It was a loft, with the bedroom platform overlooking the living room.

Hankins came home from the hospital, the baby in a car carrier the hospital staff had gotten for her. She opened the door, put the baby down and locked the door behind her.

"Don't get used to this place, brat. You ain't staying long. You're heading to a new home and you're going to make me a little wealthier."

"You're right about the new home part," Argus said, stepping out from a coat closet, his gun drawn. Hankins saw the silencer and broke out in a cold sweat.

The door opened on the second-floor landing. One way lead to the stairs, the other to her loft bedroom.

"You!" she said, trying to open her purse.

Argus yanked it from her before she could get to the gun inside.

Argus kept the gun by his hip but pointed at her. "Sit down and shut up."

Hankins obeyed and sat at her desk, her hand slowly moving toward a drawer handle.

"Don't bother. I already removed the revolver." Argus put a stack of adoption papers in front of her. "Sign all three of these."

Hankins read over the papers. "So, the Greenes hired you, huh? They'll never get away with this. I'll squeal that I signed under duress the moment I get into court. Because these won't hold up if I'm dead, so I know you won't kill me."

"You took their child from them, so it seems only fitting that you give them another."

"I won't do it. I'm not signing."

Argus reached forward and pressed a spot on her sternum and the new mother screamed in pain. The baby, who had been sleeping, stirred. Argus put his finger over his mouth and the adults were quiet. After about a minute, the baby was sound asleep again.

"If you don't sign, that pain will just be a warm up."

Hankins glared, gritted her teeth and took the pen. "Fine."

"Sign it as Madeleine Hankins."

"Whatever. I'm gonna let everyone know exactly how this came about, you know."

"That's your prerogative. Now we make a little video," Argus said, putting a digital camera on the table and making a big show of turning it on.

"What? Now you want me to say how I killed their son and I'm giving them my baby to make up for it. Dream on," she said, taking the memory card out and snapping it in half, then throwing the camera across the room. "You can kill me, but I'll never say that."

"No need. You already did," Argus said, pointing to a spy pen sticking out of his black coat's pocket. "We'll just edit out the start and the end and it will do just fine. The video will remove any doubt about the Greenes' innocence in the death of their son."

"You don't actually think that pathetic video will be enough to explain away my death? Don't you think it will be a little suspicious with me with a bullet in my head and immediately after those morons suddenly have my baby? You don't think the cops will come around asking questions?"

"Not really, especially since you signed your suicide note."

"What are you talking about?"

"You only read the first page of the adoption agreement, which are the first two documents you signed. The last page of the third one basically tells about what you did to all those people you stole children from. I listed all the people you gave children to. I imagine the cops will track down the real parents with the missing children database and DNA testing. I love how you say how your guilt made you include your lawyer partner-in-crimes' files and that this confession along with giving your child to the Greene's is the one good thing you did with your life. Now you can end it all with a clear conscience since you already dropped off the baby to her new parents."

"One big problem, smart guy. I ain't gonna kill myself, so your whole plan falls apart right there," she said smugly.

"I guess you're right. You win."

Hankins laughed and stood up, barely noticing Argus flick his wrist so a noose fell over her head and around her neck. The other end was tied to some pipes that ran across the ceiling. The bedroom loft had no rail so Argus simply pushed the kidnapping baby killer over the edge.

Hankins didn't even have time for a scream, only a gasp of surprise, as her body fell and her neck snapped, instantly killing her.

Argus checked to make sure she was dead. The baby had slept through it all. The hitman picked up the carrier, the Greenes' pre-signed copy of the adoption agreement and left everything else. Shirley and Jerry were already in town and they had everything that the baby would need.

Shirley Greene had been hoping for another boy, but Argus knew she'd be okay with the girl. The only thing she really wanted was for the baby to be healthy and her mother to be finally dead.

KILLING GRANDFATHERS

"I can't let you in here." Barber was more mountain than man and Argus believed the bouncer.

"But I was invited." The bouncer only narrowed his eyes at the thinly veiled joke. "I was asked to meet somebody here."

"And why is that?" Barber said.

"Because he thought it was a safe place to meet."

"Plasma is very safe."

Plasma was the name of the nightclub. Its theme was to cater to people who pretended they were vampyres, at least that was what they liked to portray. If Argus's reconnaissance was anywhere near the mark, there wasn't much pretending going on.

"And how safe do you think people would feel if I let you in carrying all those guns and knives?" Argus started to open up to his mouth, but Barber cut him off. "Save the denials. You have an excellent tailor but you're packing a small armory. A well-tailored suit is not enough to fool me. I've been doing this for a long time."

A very long time if the stories were to be believed. Argus had heard that this bouncer had done the same job for a place called Bulfinche's Pub during prohibition. Bulfinche's was another place that had so many stories told about it that it couldn't all be believed, but Argus still hoped they were true. The people at that bar had stopped the apocalypse and helped a succubus escape from Hell.

Argus had resigned himself to the fact that the Devil would one day take his soul, but sometimes he allowed himself a glimmer of hope that he could get out of the deal. Visiting Bulfinche's Pub seemed like it might be a good idea to help out with that if he could ever find the place. Of course, Barber had even more stories about him including that he had been around North America back before America existed and had later worked on some sort of mystical version of the Underground Railroad. Why somebody rumored to have such a ridiculous amount of personal power was working as a bouncer instead of running New York City from the shadows was an interesting question, just not one for today.

"How safe do you think our patrons are going to feel if I just let people walk in packing weapons?"

"Probably not as safe as they would like. Although I find it interesting that you made a woman ahead of me take her crucifix off. Doesn't seem like much of a weapon."

Barber had what was possibly a glimpse of a grin or perhaps his lip merely twitched. "It had some sharp edges."

"So, what do you suggest? What do you usually do in cases like this?" Argus said.

"Under other circumstances, I'd send you packing. You wouldn't believe the number of people who come to a place like this with the intention of trying to kill a vampyre," Barber said. The big man seemed to be looking for a reaction.

All Argus gave him was an answer. "I might."

"But in your case, I'd consider making an exception because one of our patrons warned us ahead of time and asked for you to be let in."

"Excellent." Argus started to take a step but the man mountain wasn't about to move to make way for Mohammed let alone a hitman.

"I'll let you in as soon as we address the issue of your armaments. If you would be willing to check your weapons with me, I'll allow you to enter in. If not, you can go somewhere else."

"Are you giving me your personal guarantee that my gear will be returned in the same condition and that I will get it back when I leave?"

"Provided you don't cause any trouble, you'll get everything back in the same condition when you exit."

"Okay, but is there a private area we could do this?"

"Of course. Follow me."

Barber motioned Argus through the door to a side room that had a safe door that was bigger than the one that led into the room.

Barber placed his hand on the pad to the side of the safe and the safe door popped open.

"Pretty high-tech for a nightclub."

"Cuts down on people trying to break in if the only way to open it is my handprint," Barber said.

"It just means that someone would have to get a hold of your hands to do it," Argus said with a smile.

The look Barber graced the hitman with suggested the mere idea was incredibly stupid and ridiculous. The bouncer pulled out a lockbox and opened the lid. Argus started placing gun after gun and then blade after blade into the box. It almost wasn't big enough.

"All done," Argus said.

"Not quite. You still have a throwing dart hidden in your boxers. And a flask."

"Impressive, all without even frisking me. How do you do it?"

Barber just stared at him and didn't say a word as Argus reached inside his pants and pulled out a two-inch dart and held it up.

"Usually I carry a much bigger one." Barber just continued to stare silently. "Tough room. Mind if I keep the flask? I won't drink in front of your paying customers." Argus took the cap off and took a slug. "See? Harmless."

"It's holy water and it stays in the box."

Argus looked at the flask, shrugged, then took a much bigger sip. "Can hardly taste the blessing at all."

Argus closed the flask and placed it in the box, closed the lid and Barber placed it back in the safe.

The large bouncer walked the hitman out into the club proper.

"Aren't you going to tell me you're going to be keeping an eye on me or something like that?" Argus said.

"I won't insult your intelligence by stating the obvious."

"Appreciate it."

Argus should have felt at home. After all, he wasn't dressed much differently from many of the people in the club. He wore a long black leather trench coat and dark sunglasses at midnight.

Even his hair was black, although he came by that naturally, unlike some of the clubgoers. They all seemed fascinated with death, as if they were playing a game with the Reaper. Argus had learned long ago that death was no game, but if it was, he would've made the All-Star team for sure.

Many of the people in the club were pretending to be vampyres, down to the fangs, but most seemed about as deadly as a Chihuahua. Many had fangs, only some of which were bought. People didn't realize the danger all around them or maybe that was part of the thrill, a gazelle going to the lions' watering hole and knowing they made it home alive.

Some folks were reveling in the adoration of people who at least believed they were real creatures of the night. Others just went about their business.

There was one man at a table in the corner who seemed as uncomfortable as a nun attending a stripper convention. He nodded toward the hitman and Argus walked over to the table.

"So glad you could make it," the man in the horn-rimmed glasses said, extending his hand to be shook. After Argus ignored it, he awkwardly put it back down

"Move over one seat."

"Why does the seat matter?"

"That one has its back against the wall and has a better view of the club. Move."

"Oh, hitman. Right." The man smiled, revealing long and pointed incisors as he scooted over to the next chair.

"Hope you don't mind my pick of venue." Argus didn't answer, so the vampyre in the horn-rimmed glasses kept talking to fill the silence. "I knew Layla ran a tight ship, so I figured we'd be safe in here. Plus, if you don't believe me and think I'm crazy, spending some time here might convince you otherwise."

"You mean there are people who haven't bought your story about being a vampyre?"

The vamp couldn't tell if Argus was being serious or sarcastic. "You believe me? Well, I wouldn't have before this happened."

"I've killed things that most people wouldn't believe were real.

So, let me get this straight – you want me to kill the person that made you into this?" Argus said.

"No. That wouldn't make any sense. That'd only be about revenge. Besides my wife is the one who turned me. We've been married a few years and I guess she thought I was getting boring, so she went out to sleep in greener pastures so to speak. One of her lovers was a vampyre. He turned her and then she turned me, although I guess she did it more for poops and giggles. She thought it might make me exciting again. The truth is, I like being boring. I like going to work, then coming home. I like going out with friends. I didn't need to go skydiving or bungee cord jumping to enjoy life. Now I can't go out during the day. I'm probably going to lose my job. If it wasn't for this place serving blood, I don't know what I'd have to do to get it."

"Hold on. Are you saying this club actually serves human blood?" The vamp in the horn-rimmed glasses nodded. "Where do they get it?"

"Volunteers. Some donate for free, some get paid. Layla - she's the owner - used to be a social worker before she became one of the undead. I guess this is her way of helping out the rest of us. It's not like you see on TV. You don't turn into a vampyre and become evil. Vamps become powerful and the impulses they may have been repressing because of consequences from society can rise to the surface. That's what happened with my wife. She actually goes out hunting with her new boyfriend and his posse."

"Posse?"

"Gang? Crew? Clan? I don't know what you're supposed to call them. All I know is they hurt people to feed. My wife keeps inviting me to go along, but I'd really rather watch Netflix."

"So, what it boils down to is you want me to kill the guy your wife is sleeping with. That's not really the type of job I take."

"It's not about that. Okay, maybe it's a little about that, but only a tiny bit. Hanging out here, I've learned a little bit about how vampyres work. There's an actual vampyre handbook, believe it or not. Helps those of us unwittingly turned to survive. There's all sorts of different kinds of vampyres, all because of some curse back in the Bible thanks to some guy who killed his brother."

"Cain?" Argus said.

The man in the horn-rimmed glasses nodded. "Seems he was cursed to walk the Earth and he's still around. Turns out if anyone tries to hurt him, the curse turns them into a first-generation vampyre. Then they can go out and sire up to seven more generations of vampyres. The seventh-generation is neutered and can't propagate by turning others. Killing the person who made me a vampyre won't lift the curse. But killing the first-generation vampyre in my lineage will lift the curse from everyone on down the line, including me."

"So how are you so sure your wife's lover…"

"Hank."

"Hank is the first-generation vampyre?"

"I can't be a hundred percent sure. After all, I didn't see it happen, but I heard him claim that was the case when my wife tried to convince me to join their posse and run around killing innocent people. Hank said he was ashamed that I shared his bloodline. Then he tried to kill me, but turns out I could run faster than him."

"Each vampyre bloodline has different powers and abilities. What can yours do?"

"Pretty boring actually. We're strong and fast. I can jump really high, but we can't turn into bats or wolves or anything cool like that. But we can turn into a mist, but it's hard to move. We just sort of drift slowly, but it's enough that we can't get shot or stabbed while we're mist. I can't be out when the sun is, holy water burns me, and garlic messes me up pretty bad. Although I do have food allergies so I don't know if it's related to the vampyre bloodline because gluten and dairy does the same thing."

"You realize that if this guy is never alone, I'd have to take out him and his… posse, which includes your wife."

"If at all possible try not to kill her. Once Hank is dead, Dolores will go back to being a human again."

"Sparing her may not be possible if she's with Hank, especially if she presents a danger to myself or other people. You have thoughts of a reconciliation?"

"Hell, no. She cheated on me and turned me into one of the undead. We're through, but I just want to divorce her, not have her killed, you know?"

Argus nodded and took a bullet out of his pocket and placed it on the table in front of the vamp. It had the name Bob Lager engraved on it.

"Here's how this works. You swear that everything you told me is true but if I find out you've lied to me then this bullet's coming back for you. Understood?"

Bob nodded and picked up the bullet. "I swear it's all true." The vamp pulled his hand away like it had been burnt and dropped the bullet on the table.

Argus scooped it up so fast that if someone watching had blinked they would've missed it. The hitman put it back in his pocket.

"Add silver to the list of things that can hurt your bloodline. Now on to the matter of payment. To do this job for you I require two hundred and sixty thousand dollars in advance."

Bob gave a long and slow whistle. "That's a lot of moola. I don't have that kind of money. I can get you fifty K."

"Bob, this isn't *Let's Make A Deal* or a negotiation. And you're lucky you said that after you swore on the bullet or I might have to shoot you on principle for lying to me. The new price is $297,628.14."

"That's an awful specific amount," Bob said, his brows creasing.

"It's the exact amount in your 401(k) and savings account at the close of the market today."

"But that's all I have."

"All the money you have. But you know what you don't have now? A human heartbeat. Or the ability to go out during the day and feel sunshine your face. What you do have are some pretty neat superpowers and a hunger for human blood. How long do you think before you give in and do something to hurt somebody else? Can you live with yourself when that happens? You don't need *me* to do this. In theory, you should be just as strong as Hank and you said you're faster than he is. Why don't you kill him yourself?"

"I've never even been in a real fight. I don't know how to kill somebody, let alone a vampyre. He'd kill me."

"Exactly." Argus slid a piece of paper over to Bob. "You have one day to transfer the money into that account but you better hurry because in twenty-five hours it won't exist."

"So, once I give you this money, you'll kill the vampyre that did this to me?"

"I will."

A chair flew through the air towards Argus, but the hitman ducked and it smashed against the wall where his head had been a moment before.

"You're actually talking about killing a vampyre, here of all places? Stinking human! I'm gonna kill you instead," said a vampyre in black leather pants, a gray T-shirt with the sleeves torn off. That was covered up by a black leather trench coat, which also was missing sleeves. The studded collar around his neck and blue hair up in a Mohawk was reminiscent of a bygone era.

Argus looked accusingly at Bob who put his hands up defensively. "We do have good hearing."

Argus flipped the table up towards the vampyre who kicked the center of it, splitting it and kept coming towards the hitman.

Argus reached his thumb and index finger along the inside of his mouth. The hitman pulled out a metal spike wrapped in cotton and threw it into the vamp's left eye, which exploded in a ball of fire. He was reaching into the other side of his mouth with his other hand when suddenly Barber was there between the pair. The mammoth bouncer held a hand palm up towards Argus and grabbed the vampyre with the blue Mohawk by his throat and lifted him up.

"Vincenzo, you know the rules. No violence in Plasma or the surrounding neighborhood," Barber said.

"That bastard took my eye!"

"After you attacked him. The man was just defending himself. If you had a beef you should have taken it outside the neighborhood. Now you're banned."

Barber tossed Vincenzo across the room to land on the floor in front of a couple of other vamp bouncers. They grabbed the vamp with the Mohawk by his shoulders and dragged him out. The man mountain crossed his arms over his chest and turned his attention to Argus.

"Taste good?"

Argus shrugged. "I don't go anywhere weaponless. I figured the flask with the holy water wouldn't fool you, so I had a backup dart with a tiny spot coated like a Q-tip, which absorbed some holy water when I drank it. Figured it might help keep me alive if it came to that. It did."

"In the interest of keeping you alive even longer, I am asking you to leave."

"Just as soon as I get all my stuff back."

"I said you could have it back if you didn't cause any trouble."

"I didn't start anything. If I don't get what you told me you'd give back, that could change."

Barber laughed. "With that one little metal spike, no bigger than my pinky, coated in holy water?"

The big vampyre bent down to where the spike had been thrown free of the eyeball by the resulting fireball. Barber picked it up and placed the still wet end onto the middle of his forehead. "Holy water and religious artifacts don't bother me. I can go out in the day too. So, if you want trouble, I'll make sure you get plenty."

Argus stood up and tilted his head back so he could stare up into Barber's nostrils. "Again, give me back what is mine and all's well. If not, I guess you'll find out what other tricks I have up my sleeve. Metaphorically speaking of course. But I'm not worried."

"No?" Barber said.

"Not a bit. Because you gave me your word and you strike me as a man of his word. And I've heard that you were a member of the League of Shadows back in the Depression days. Can't imagine anyone associated with that group being an oath breaker, can you?"

Barber smiled and chuckled then slapped Argus on the back, almost knocking him to the floor. "Let's get you your stuff. I like you. You got guts. That doesn't mean I want to see you back anytime soon."

"I'm okay with that too."

One might think that it would be hard to track down creatures of the night and you'd be right. Then again, it's a challenge to track anybody down, but it's made much easier when the person isn't trying to hide.

Turns out, his target's full name was Hank Scarlet. Not the name his parents gave him, but apparently, the one he chose for himself. Hank had it legally changed and took out credit cards under it. And used said credit cards. Hank didn't have a job, but that still didn't stop him ordering expensive clothes and toys off the Internet on a regular basis. But he never had a late payment, mainly thanks to his ability to extort and steal money from his victims, which he then used to pay off his credit card debt.

Good old Hank must've considered himself quite the ladies' man because his "posse" consisted of five women and only two other men. One of the men owned an apartment on the Upper East Side and had a trust fund which gave them all a place to live.

Argus thought about hitting them at the apartment but decided against it. Too many variables he couldn't control and too great a risk for bystanders to get hurt. There was also no way he could guess with any accuracy where they would hunt next, so he set up his trap in the alley outside their building.

This hit wasn't going to be something typical. He'd learned a few things when he took out McMillian the unkillable zombie and a lot more since. The things that go bump in the night, for the most part, could be killed. It just took extra planning and preparation. A lot of it. Plus, the vampyres were guilty of overconfidence and most of them couldn't conceive that a mere mortal could ever hurt them.

Argus planned to offer them a victim close to home, but he had to make himself seem harmless and helpless. To accomplish this, he ditched the trench coat and dark sunglasses. Instead, he put on a pair of ratty jeans, beat up sneakers and a pair of horned rim glasses not entirely dissimilar to his client's. He wore a dress shirt buttoned all the way to the collar without a tie. He even made sure half of it was untucked. And to top it all off literally, he put his hair up in a man bun. He stopped short of a pocket protector as he felt it was dated and overkill. He snuck in and set up video surveillance in the lobby of the building and waited in the alley on the other side of the building once the sun went down.

Hank and his posse weren't early risers. It was ten minutes after eleven before they finally made their way out the door.

Argus came out of the alley holding a book and walking while reading. He made sure to appear as if he wasn't looking where he was going and smashed right into Hank. The vamp reacted by knocking the book from his hands into the street and shoving Argus back onto the sidewalk.

"Hey, watch it, buddy. I'm walking here," Argus said in a higher than normal voice that had nasal tones added in for good measure.

"You get a death wish buddy? Cause we will be willing to help you out with that," Hank said.

Argus gave a disbelieving snort and scurried over to where his book had plopped, landing paper down in a puddle between the curb and a car tire. He picked it up with a horrified look upon his face, his eyes wide and his jaw dropped low, before turning to glare at Hank.

"I'll have you know that this is a rare first edition *Souls on Fire* by John L French and you've ruined it. Its current value is $37.23. If you know what's good for you, you'll reimburse me for damaging this classic work of literature immediately," Argus whined, waving the book in the vampyre's face.

Hank laughed and looked at his fellow vamps, all of whom were also smiling and laughing. "Yeah? What are you going to do if I don't?"

"Well, I'll have you know that my second cousin, who I grew up across the street from and who I am very close to, is a personal injury attorney. I will sue you."

Hank narrowed his brows, having difficulty believing what he was hearing. "You're going to sue me? Over some book?"

"Indeed. Your only way to avoid this severe consequence is to pay me what I'm owed."

Hank laughed. "I'm not paying you anything."

"Then you leave me no choice." Argus took a pad and pen out of his pocket and posed as if he was about to write. "I insist you give me your personal information so I know who to name in the lawsuit. And I must warn you. I will be adding in money for emotional distress. I was at the most exciting part."

Hank looked at his so-called posse of vampyres and grinned. They grinned right back but were all careful to keep their fangs hidden.

"All right, I don't want that, now do I? Let me give you what you're owed. Come into this alley over here and I'll pay you."

Argus squinted and looked at Hank. "Why can't you pay me out here? Why do you want to go in an alley? Do you have some nefarious purpose in mind?"

"Nefarious?" Hank smirked but put a friendly arm around Argus' shoulders. "No, nothing like that. I just don't want any undercover police to see me handing you money and think we were making some sort of a drug deal."

"Hmm." Argus stroked his chin, then straightened his horn-rimmed glasses. "I suppose that makes sense. Fine. Get your wallet out."

Argus walked into the alley, the vampyres following behind him and licking their lips.

Argus went a little bit more than halfway down the alley and turned around. "This is far enough away from the street for you?"

"It'll do. But we're not to give you any money," Hank said, smiling so his fangs showed. The other seven members of his posse stood behind him, effectively blocking any exit through the mouth of the alley.

"That's okay. I didn't figure you would." Argus clicked the top of the pen and several things happened all at once. UV lamps flicked on from above and at the mouth of the alley. Fire sprinklers spraying blessed liquid, covering the alley in a fine mist of holy water. Argus reached behind a dumpster to pull out the largest custom-made shotgun any of the vampyres had ever seen before.

The hitman fired three times, peppering all eight vampyres with a mix of silver and garlic soaked in holy water. The holy water sprinklers made their skin looked like they had bathed in acid and the UV lamps were causing their exposed skin to smoke.

All eight vampyres hit the cement with a combination of screams and sizzles.

Hank leapt above Argus only to have his head sliced by some very thin silver wire. Argus stepped forward and put shotgun blasts directly into the heads of five of the writhing vampyres. The hitman missed a sixth. The shot hadn't missed where he was aiming. The target had just moved faster than the shotgun blast could travel. The woman then leapt at him lightning fast. Argus was smashed into the alley wall as she ripped the shotgun out of his hands and smashed it in half. Argus pulled a crucifix out of his pocket.

"Crosses work for everybody, but other religious symbols only work if the person believes," she mocked.

As the vampyre rushed at him, the hitman rammed the pointed end of the crucifix into her throat and out through her spine. An instant after, her neck and head caught fire.

"You believe? How?" the female vamp asked, her words each sizzling as if spoken on a meat packed grill.

How could a hitman believe in God? Being raised Catholic had drilled the basics into him. And since Argus had met the Devil, in his mind it kind of proved the existence of God, despite what Nick would try to tell people otherwise.

From the small of his back, Argus pulled a long silver coated blade and decapitated the woman whose head was on fire, then sliced the head in half before it hit the ground.

That left just two vampyres, Loretta and Hank. Loretta was curled up in a ball and Hank had gotten to his feet and growled as he faced Argus.

"You're a dead man."

Hank turned into a mist which moved slowly towards Argus. The Soul for Hire ran, flipped open the top of a rather large dumpster and jumped inside. The mist tried to follow the man then realized it was a mistake but it was too late.

Argus had strapped himself in, then flipped the switch on a specially rigged military surplus small jet engine. The mist was caught in the intake and Hank was sucked through the turbines and spit out beneath the dumpster into a stream of holy water.

By this point the dumpster was straining against the chains and anchors Argus had installed in the cement and was two feet off the ground. Argus flipped off the switch and it crashed to the ground. He let out the deep breath he had been holding and climbed out. He rolled the dumpster to the side. Hank had reformed underneath the dumpster, but without skin or hair. Argus sliced his head off with the blade, then sliced that in two before turning his attention to Loretta.

The barrels of holy water that were fueling the fire sprinklers were down to drips. The vamp's head and hands were a gooey mess, but her clothing had provided some protection from the UV rays and the blessed liquid.

"So, Loretta, what are you going to do after this?" Argus asked, clicking his pen and shutting off the UV lamps.

"What am I going to do? You mean after I kill you? I'm going to go out and find the nearest person, drain their blood and heal, then rebuild my family."

"You mean get back together with your husband?"

"Hell, no. I'll be the head of my new family. I'll be the one turning people into vampyres so they will be obeying me. I'm going to run the show. The city ain't never seen anything like what I'm about to bring down on it."

"Very ambitious. Two problems with that. Hank is dead, so you're not a vampyre anymore. Maybe with the right medical care, you might be able to heal from those wounds, but you're not going to be turning anybody else undead."

"Bullshit. I ain't feeling no pain. No way I'm human again."

The hitman shook his head. "The reason you're not feeling pain - despite the shape your body is in - is because you've gone into shock. And some of your sensory nerves may have been entirely melted away."

Loretta absorbed what she was told slowly. "What's the second thing?"

Argus swung the blade, neatly decapitating the burned and dissolving woman. "This."

Argus quickly moved the bodies into the dumpster, then took down the sprinklers and the UV lights and put them in it as well. He pulled out a pair of overalls from inside a garbage can and put them on along with a baseball cap.

He walked to the corner where he parked a garbage truck and then backed into the alley, loaded up the dumpster then drove slowly away.

THE MONSTER IN THE CLOSET

"You really don't want me to check under your bed or in your closet for monsters?" James Porter said, having trouble believing his ears.

His six-year-old son Johnny stood there and shook his head.

"So, you've given up on the idea that a monster killed your baby sister Sarah?" James said.

"Nope. But I'm doing what you said. I'm manning up and taking care of the problem myself," Johnny said.

The father sighed. "What happened to Sarah was a tragedy but the medical examiner said it was SIDS, not a monster."

Johnny rolled his eyes. No less than ten grownups had explained SIDS to him. He understood the first time.

"Dad, I know what I saw and you don't believe me. The monster said it was a Bugabear and that it was going to kill Sarah. I told you that the day before she died. If you believed me, maybe my baby sister would still be alive. The monster said it would be back for me tonight and you didn't believe me again," Johnny said.

James gritted his teeth and got down on one knee so he could look at his son directly in the eyes. "Johnny, you have a vivid imagination. It's one of the best things about you, but you have to realize what happened was just a nightmare. There are no such thing as monsters. What happened to Sarah wasn't your fault."

"I know. It was the Bugabear's. And yours and mom's a little bit for not believing me."

"Johnny, your mother and I love you very much. I think we may have to arrange to have you talk to somebody so you can work out this problem."

"I already talked to somebody and he is going to help me take care of the problem."

James tilted his head quizzically. "Somebody at school? One of your friends?"

"I guess he's a friend. He helps people like me."

James nodded his head, knowing that the school had provided grief counseling for his son and assumed that's who Johnny meant. "Now get in bed and go to sleep."

Johnny climbed beneath the covers. His father tucked the blankets around his shoulders, kissed him on the forehead then left.

But Johnny didn't go to sleep. He waited quietly in the dark for two hours.

His mother, Janice, came in to kiss him good night and whisper that she loved him. Johnny pretended to be asleep.

A few minutes later his parents turned off all the lights and went to bed themselves.

Johnny waited another twenty minutes before getting up and opening his closet, where Vince Argus had been hiding all night long

"Thanks, kid. It was getting cramped in there."

"You can really kill the monster that killed my sister, Mr. Argus?" Johnny said.

"That's the plan, kid."

"I was kind of hoping for a guarantee for my hundred dollars."

"Kid, getting me for a hundred bucks is the best deal you'll ever make in your life. Your parents catch me in here and that won't even pay my bail." Argus took out a net and set it up on the walls, ceiling, and floor. "And provided your monster doesn't show up in the next ten minutes, I'd say we had a pretty good shot at ending it and making sure it doesn't hurt any more kids."

"Including me," Johnny said.

Argus smiled. "Especially you, kid."

"Why did you believe me when no other grown-ups did?" Johnny said.

"Probably because I've seen and done things that they haven't. That and you were very convincing. And stubborn."

"I didn't like the bullet part."

"Sorry kid. Everyone's got to promise they're telling the truth. That's how it works. I don't make exceptions for anybody."

"I don't like being the bait either."

The hitman shrugged. "Without you, this plan falls apart. The monster won't show if you're not here."

Johnny bit his bottom lip and nodded.

Argus left one portion of the floor uncovered by the net and drew a chalk circle around himself.

"I've never seen chalk that could write like that on carpet," Johnny said.

"It's special chalk. That little bit probably used up your hundred bucks right there."

"So, the monster won't be able to tell you're there?"

"He won't be able to smell me or sense me using magic." Argus had gotten better at triggering a spell circle. There was no need to use a weapon to turn it on. All he really had to do was hit a target which he did by throwing a penny at the chalk line. "However, if your parents walk in they'll be able to see me just fine. Now pretend you're asleep."

"The monster knows that I know it's coming. Wouldn't it expect me to be awake and scared?"

"Good point, kid. Pretend to be scared."

"I don't have to pretend."

The minutes turned into hours and Argus thought that perhaps he'd misjudged Johnny and the kid had made the whole thing up, but he stayed. He'd taken the job and he'd see it through either way.

When the monster showed up, he was silent and came in through the window. Although that wasn't really the best description. The window itself wasn't open, but the creature came in through the cracks. It just flowed through the empty spaces, as if it and the window had reached an agreement that they would both ignore the laws of physics for a few moments.

The creature crept over to the child's bedside and loomed over the boy, waiting until Johnny opened his eyes and looked right at him.

"Your time is up, child."

"No, yours is." At the sound of the voice, the bugabear tried to bolt, but Argus had already triggered the spring loaders on the net and it closed up with the nursery monster inside. Argus grabbed the ends and made it tighter.

"Human fool! This plastic net won't hold me." To prove his point the creature - which looked like a shortened hairy man with a nose that was practically a beak - used long black claws to shred the net, but it didn't work out as planned. Instead, the claws broke off and its skin began to smoke.

"It's not a plastic net. It's just coated with it. The net itself is made from iron, something your kind don't deal too well with. The plastic was to camouflage the iron so you didn't realize you had walked into a trap."

"Human, why do you do this to me? I've done nothing to you or yours."

"Did you kill this boy's baby sister?"

The nursery monster cackled uproariously. "Oh yes. Her essence was pure and delicious. The boy is not quite as pure, but there is more essence to devour."

"Not tonight. Not ever again."

The monster cackled again. "Stupid human. Children are immune to our mind control, but adults are not. The boy's mother watched me one time when I visited the girl. I told her to go back to bed and forget about it and she obeyed. *Now you are going to open this net, take that gun, put it in your mouth and pull the trigger. Twice.*"

The Soul for Hire froze and slipped the gun out of his holster and brought it up towards his mouth.

"Mr. Argus, no! Snap out of it!"

Argus winked at the kid and turned the gun towards the nursery monster.

"Impossible! The child's words shouldn't have been enough to free you from my control. Otherwise, the screams of a dying child would never be ignored by a parent."

"You're right. The kid didn't break your control because I was never under it," Argus said.

"But how…" The nursery monster bent his head forward and looked through the gaps in the net, then tilted his head to the side. "You are marked by Hell. It gives you resistance to mind control."

"Yeah, not immune, but it will take someone better than you to put me under. One of the good side effects of my deal."

The monster snickered. "That solves the problem then. I invoke the Pantheon Accord. As I'm only being true to my nature, I am immune from any and all persecution for it by any of the signers of the Accord. That includes the Pit. But I am not unreasonable. Once you set me free, I will relinquish my claim on the boy."

"I think you misunderstand. I made a deal with Hell, but I'm not the Pit's bitch. I don't work for Hell. I work for the kid and he says you die for what you did to his sister.

"I see. *Come to me.*"

"I thought we already established that won't work on me."

The nursery monster cackled. "What makes you think I was speaking to you?"

Janice Porter ran in the bedroom door, her eyes glazed over. James Porter ran after his wife.

"Honey, what's wrong?" James asked, then he saw the strange man in the black trench coat and dark sunglasses holding a net with some sort of man creature in it while his son crouched on his bed. "What the hell is going on here?"

"*Woman, shut him up,*" the monster said. Janice punched her husband in the mouth and then brought her knee up into his groin. It didn't knock him out, but it did make him fall down to the floor.

"*Woman, kill your son for me,*" the nursery monster said.

Janice leapt forward to do its bidding

Johnny went over one side of the bed and then underneath it. "Mommy, it's me, Johnny. Stop it. Don't hurt me."

It was too late. The woman grabbed her son's legs and pulled the boy out from beneath the bed. The violence with which she did it, tore the boy's nails which were digging into the carpet in a futile attempt to stay put.

"You have a choice human. Save your employer or…"

Bang.

Argus fired an iron bullet between the monster's eyes, then let go of the net. The hitman pulled out a knife and tossed it at the boy's mother.

"No!" the husband shouted, seeing the blade flying toward his wife.

At the last instant, it flipped so the hilt hit her between the eyes. The shock of the impact was enough to break the monster's control and the bugabear's death a moment later was enough to end it completely.

The boy's father struggled to his feet just in time to watch the little hairy man with a beak turn to dust.

"How?" James asked.

"When I killed it, all the magic went out of its body. When that happens to something that old, there's no body, only dust." Argus opened the closet door and took out a small portable vacuum cleaner. He turned it on and began sucking up the ash.

"You brought a gun, a knife, and a vacuum cleaner?"

"It pays to be prepared. I had no way of knowing how old the thing was, but I find it's always best to dispose of the remains thoroughly to make sure the thing doesn't come back. And to make sure there's no evidence for forensics."

"Why did my wife attack us?"

Johnny had gone back under the bed and out the other side to hide behind Argus. His mother was stunned, with a new bruise on her face but didn't remember any of it.

"Johnny, what's going on? Why are you acting like you're scared of me?"

"It wasn't her fault. The thing got its psychic hooks into her when it killed your daughter."

"That thing killed Sarah? You mean Johnny wasn't making it up?"

Argus nodded. "You've got a good boy. You should listen to him."

"I told you I wasn't lying, but you wouldn't believe me. If it wasn't for Mr. Argus I would've died too."

"Because I don't believe you, you went out and hired a hitman? How does a six-year-old even figure out how to hire a hitman? Young man, you are in such trouble right now."

Argus paused his vacuuming and looked at James Porter. "No, he is not. Johnny is smart and more resourceful than most adults. He managed to save his own life and possibly your wife's soul. She had to do whatever the creature asked. From what I understand after they kill a child they get a sick twisted thrill trying to make another one with the mother."

Janice Porter shivered and James Porter's eyes went wide and he moved to embrace his wife then the two of them brought Johnny into the hug.

Argus finished up the last of the vacuuming and knelt down in front of the boy.

"Kid, you did good. And if anyone gives you trouble again, you know to reach me." He looked at Johnny's father when he said that. Then turned so he was looking at both the parents. "I was never here. Are we clear on that?"

The parents nodded nervously.

"Thank you, Mr. Argus," Johnny said.

"You're welcome."

"You were right. That was the best hundred dollars I ever spent."

"You took a hundred dollars from our son?" Janice Porter screamed, but shut up quickly when Argus turned to stare up at her.

Johnny handed Argus a tiny green blanket. "This is what I used to sleep with to help keep the monsters away, but I don't think I need it anymore. I want you to have it. Maybe it will help keep your monsters away."

Argus took the blanket from the child and messed the boy's hair

"Thanks, kid." Argus took off his sunglasses and put them on Johnny. "Here, these are for you."

When Argus looked at the parents as he was leaving with uncovered eyes, the sight made them shiver and take a step back.

PATRICK THOMAS is the author of almost 40 books including the beloved fantasy humor Murphy's Lore series, which includes *Tales From Bulfinche's Pub, Fools' Day, Through The Drinking Glass, Shadow Of The Wolf, Redemption Road, Bartender Of The Gods, Nightcaps* and *Empty Graves* — as well as the future space adventures *Startenders* and *Constellation Prize.*

The Murphy's Lore After Hours spin-offs star the half pixie/ogre Terrorbelle (*Fairy With A Gun, Fairy Rides The Lightning);* the former demon-possessed serial killer Agent Karver of the Department of Mystic Affairs *(Dead To Rites, Rites of Passage);* the cursed magí Hex *(By Darkness Cursed and BY Invocation Only);* Vince Argus, the Soul For Hire *(Greatest Hits);* and Negral, a forgotten Sumerian god who works as Hell's Detective *(Lore & Dysorder* and *Bullets & Brimstone).*

Co-Written with John French and Diane Raetz, his Mystic Investigators paranormal mystery series includes *Bullets & Brimstone, From The Shadows* and *Once More Upon A Time. Assassin's Ball,* his first mystery, is also co-written with John French.

He also wrote the steampunk *As The Gears Turn* and the space epic *Exile & Entrance.* He co-edited *New Blood* and *Hear Them Roar* and was an editor for the magazines *Fantastic Stories of the Imagination* and *Pirate Writings.*

Patrick's darkly humorous advice column Dear Cthulhu has been running since 2005 and includes the collections *Have A Dark Day, Good Advice For Bad People, Cthulhu Knows Best* and *What Would Cthulhu Do?*

His short stories have been featured in over fifty anthologies and more than forty-five print magazines.

A number of his books were part of the props department of the CSI television show and have been spotted on the program. Nightcaps was even thrown at a suspect's head. His urban fantasy Fairy With A Gun had been optioned for film and TV by Laurence Fishburne's Cinema Gypsy Productions. Top Men Productions has turned his Soul For Hire Story, *Act of Contrition*, into a short film.

Please drop by www.patthomas.net or follow him at I_PatrickThomas at Twitter or www.facebook.com/PatrickThomasAuthor to learn more.

No One Is Above The Lore...
Even In Hell
Hell's Detective
IT'S NOT EASY BEING HELL'S CHIEF OF POLICE.
LORE & DYSORDER
THE HELL'S DETECTIVE MYSTERIES
PATRICK THOMAS
MYSTIC INVESTIGATORS
BULLETS & BRIMSTONE
Patrick Thomas & John L. French
GHOSTMAN AND HELL'S DETECTIVE IN
TERROR
CASE OF THE MOON MANIAC
PATRICK THOMAS / BLAIR WEBB
GHOSTMAN
HELL'S DETECTIVE
DANTE
PHY'S LORE
ER HOURS
"Gritty, snappy, very dark
and very funny."
-J. L. Comeau,
Creature Feature
"Dark... and charming."
-ELLEN DATLOW
The Best Horror of the Year Vol. 4

"Delightfully Oddball"
-Dave Truesdale, SFSite

"Hilariously intelligent"
-Luke Reviews

From behind
the bar
To Across
The **STARS**

scan here for e-book

From The Murphy's Lore Universe of
PATRICK THOMAS
WWW.PATTHOMAS.NET

www.facebook.com/patrickThomasAuthor

TALES FROM THE SEA
MERMAIDS 13
Edited by
John L. French

APOCALYPSE
THIRTEEN FANTASTICAL
TALES FOR THE END OF DAYS
13
ANTHOLOGY
TACTICAL
DEFCON 1
...WARNING...
FEATURING:
MISSILE LAUNCH
EDITED BY
DIANE RAETZ

WHAT WILL THE FUTURE HOLD FOR EARTH?
FANTASTIC
13
FUTURES
ANTHOLOGY
EDITED BY
ROBERT E. WATERS
JAMES R. STRATTON

EDITED BY EDWARD J. MCFADDEN III
LUCKY
13
Thirteen Tales of
Crime & Mayhem
Good or bad, it runs out eventually.
It's all just a matter of luck.
FEATURING
Trent Zelazny
Jessica McHugh
Matt Schairiti
Sarah A. Hoyt
Brady Allen
Danielle Ackley-McPhail
Patrick Thomas
Robert E. Waters
G. Elmer Munson
Diane Raetz
Georgina Morales
John L. French
Michael Laimo

IT'S A CRIME TO MISS THESE GREAT STORIES!

from author
John L. French

WWW.PADWOLF.COM